Library of
Davidson College

THE DECADENT CONSCIOUSNESS

A HIDDEN ARCHIVE OF LATE VICTORIAN LITERATURE

FORTY-TWO RARE AND IMPORTANT TITLES
PUBLISHED IN THIRTY-SIX VOLUMES

EDITED BY

IAN FLETCHER &
JOHN STOKES

GARLAND PUBLISHING

MONOCHROMES

Ella D'Arcy

Garland Publishing, Inc., New York & London

1977

828
D214m

Bibliographical note:

This facsimile has been made from
a copy in the collection of
the Mercantile Library Association
(M328734)

Library of Congress Cataloging in Publication Data
D'Arcy, Ella.
  Monochromes.

  (The Decadent consciousness)
  Reprint of the 1895 ed. published by Roberts Bros.,
Boston, which was issued as no. 12 of Keynotes series.
  CONTENTS: The elegie.--Irremediable.--Poor Cousin
Louis. [etc.]
  I. Title. II. Series. III. Series: Keynotes
series ; 12.
PZ3.D243Mo7   [PS3507.A5945]   813'.4   76-20056
ISBN 0-8240-2754-X

83-7484
Printed in the United States of America

MONOCHROMES

MONOCHROMES

BY ELLA D'ARCY

BOSTON: ROBERTS BROS., 1895
LONDON: JOHN LANE, VIGO ST

Copyright, 1895,
BY ROBERTS BROTHERS.

University Press:
JOHN WILSON AND SON, CAMBRIDGE, U. S. A.

TO

THE CHIEF.

CONTENTS.

	PAGE
"THE ELEGIE"	11
IRREMEDIABLE	87
POOR COUSIN LOUIS	123
THE PLEASURE-PILGRIM	165
WHITE MAGIC	221
THE EXPIATION OF DAVID SCOTT	239

"THE ELEGIE."

"THE ELEGIE."

I.

"Into paint will I grind thee, O my Bride!"

Do you know how Schoenemann's "Elegie" came to be written?

This is the story.

In the summer of '40, Emil Schoenemann, then quite a young man, returned from Leipsic, where he had been studying under Brockhoff, to his native village of Klettendorf-am-Rhein. He had already written his "Traum-Bilder," those delicious fugitive thoughts which Vieth's fine rendering has since made known all over Europe; and we can trace in this early composition the warm imagination, the aspirations towards the Beautiful and the Good, and the wide, vague hopes as yet unfulfilled, which mark the history of most artists.

Schoenemann came back to the homely family, to the cottage-house with its low rooms, its tiny garden and orchard, to the beautiful Rhine country with its vineyards, wooded hills, and swiftly-flowing river, purposing to spend the summer months in a profitable solitude.

But his fame had preceded him. Every one knew of young Schoenemann's Academy successes; Herr Postmeister and Herr Schulmeister held learned discussions on the subject of his musical genius, and Herr Schumacher, who had played the 'cello in trios with Emil's father, predicted emphatically a great career for his old friend's son. But it was Harms, the organist, who did most to spread Schoenemann's glory round and about; for it was to Harms, his earliest master, that Emil had sent in affectionate remembrance a manuscript copy of the "Traum-Bilder" the preceding Christmas.

Harms became enthusiastic over this composition. All the winter it had been his constant theme for discourse. He had played portions on every piano in Klettendorf, and for miles around. He could not see an instrument without sitting down to it, asked or unasked, to demonstrate the beauties of the "Bilder." He would play a few bars, then dash his hands down upon the notes in a rush of admiration which rendered his fingers powerless, and, flinging himself round to face his audience, would call their attention in stammering words to the profundity of the thought, the subtlety of the scoring, the originality of this or that phrase, until he had roused excitement to a pitch nearly equalling his own. Then he would toss back his already grizzling head with a doglike shake, and begin the composition over again, to recommence the moment he had finished, lest inadvertently he should have slurred over one of its thousand excellences.

Yet, that Klettendorf took Schoenemann at Harms's estimate was due rather to the latter's faith, energy, and good-will, than to his skilful interpretation of his ex-pupil's work; poor Harms was but a mediocre pianist. It was reserved for Vieth to combine a just appreciation of Schoenemann's genius with a fine illustrative talent of his own. Naturally, if Harms had possessed such a talent, he would not have found himself at forty the obscure organist of a Rhine village.

Among those persons to whom he had spoken of the young composer with most warmth were the Dittenheims. Graf Dittenheim owned Klettendorf and most of the land thereabouts; he possessed across the river at Godesberg a beautiful villa, generally occupied for a few months only during the summer season. But this year the family had been there since early March, the Graefin having been ordered away from the bitter winds of Berlin. Again, as on previous occasions, Harms was allowed to give piano-lessons to the only daughter, the little Contesse Marie. But he, with the simple uncalculating generosity that distinguished him, wished her to have Schoenemann for a master instead.

"When Schoenemann comes to us in the summer," he told the Graefin, "you should not fail to give the Contesse the advantages of his help. She has a charming talent, to which I have at least done no harm; possibly even some little good. But I can take her no further. I have taught her all I know. Now, Schoenemann in six weeks will do more for her than I could in six years."

The Graefin looked at him from blue and sunken eyes. She had no interest in, or opinion on, the subject of music; it was nothing to her whether Schoenemann or Harms was her daughter's teacher. The only subject which really interested her was her own failing health; and as she looked and mused on

August's ugly face and thickset figure, where nevertheless strength and long life were so legibly written, she grew bitter against the fate which threatened to cut her off in the height of her youth and beauty. She was thirty-four, and looked twenty-six, and her passionate love of life and amusement grew keener in proportion as she seemed destined to forego them. Yet she did remember to say to her husband the next time she happened to see him, "That odd Harms wants us to have young Schoenemann to give Marie music lessons. It seems he is expected back in Klettendorf."

"So? Schoenemann?" said the Graf; "he is expected home, is he? I hear he is one of our coming men. By all means patronize him, if the little one would like it. I should be glad to help him for his father's sake. Poor Franz was a faithful servant, and a good musician himself. His touch on the violin was superb."

Thus Harms obtained the wished-for permission to bring Emil to Bellavista, and present him to the family. But on the day fixed for this ceremony it happened that a funeral service was to be celebrated in the Hofkapelle in Bonn, and that the organist was taken ill.

Harms was asked to supply his place; and, in consequence, Schoenemann found himself on the way to Bellavista alone.

It was June, gloriously sunny, three in the afternoon. It was a day for lying by woodland streams, listening to the small sounds of woodland life, seeing in fancy coy woodland nymphs peeping out from between the tree-boles. The road to Godesberg was long, dusty, and monotonous; most people would have found it insuperably dull; but Emil, who walked in the melodious company of his own thoughts, was raised far above dulness.

Every impression received through the senses became music when it reached this young man's brain. The birds sang to him, and so did the breeze in the trees. The complaining cry of a gate which a woman opened to drive through some young calves, became a whole phrase in the tone-poem growing up in his soul. A band of little children, holding hands as they advanced towards him, introduced a new train of thought. He saw himself again just such a little child as one of these, running down the village street, and listening to the tune which his iron-bound shoes rang out upon the cobbles.

The whole of this walk, or rather the emotions which it set free, has been immortalized in the descriptive opening movement of Op. 37 — so at least Vieth tells us, to whom Schoenemann confided much of his history and early experiences: the dreamy and delicious adagio was born of the rose-garden, and the impulsive passionate finale of the events that followed. But first I must describe to you this garden of Bellavista.

The highroad ran right through it; or rather, there were two separate gardens, one on either hand. In the centre of the right-hand garden, fenced off from the highway by a wire-rail and a laurel hedge, stood the house: a villa in the Italian style, that thus determined the foreign form its name should take. On the other side of the road, railed off in a similar manner, was a garden for pleasure only, extending from road to Rhine. And the view obtained from the windows of Bellavista, of rose, of myrtle, of broad-bosomed river, of upland vineyard and wood beyond, fully justified the claim set forth in the name itself.

Floating out from the two gardens, innumerable flower-perfumes blent themselves into one intoxicating whole, which was wafted far and wide, so that Schoenemann revelled in it long before he reached the open iron wicket that gave access to the house.

The path wound first between walls of glossy laurel. Then suddenly you found yourself upon an open lawn, pierced with flower-beds resembling jewels in their gorgeous colorings and geometrical shapes. Here lay a ruby, formed of black and red and crimson roses, pinned closely down to the grass in circular pattern; there climbed a clematis about a slender rod, which, massing its purple blossoms in an immense bouquet at the top, looked like a cluster of deep-hued amethysts and sapphires invisibly suspended a few feet above the ground. And scarlets, yellows, and whites, yellows and scarlets, flashed and flamed and glimmered against the greenness on every side. Yonder lay the tubing which finished in the iron standpiece of a movable fountain. It was playing now. Two broad rings of water, one above the other, revolved in contrary directions; and while the inner portion of each ring was of a glassy tenuity and smoothness, the outer edges broke up into a spray that scattered its myriad drops like diamonds in the sunshine. Continental gardens have a charm of which those who only know the green lawns and shady trees of England can form no idea. Those trees and lawns are beautiful indeed in their own peaceful way; but such a garden as Bellavista is a veritable land of enchantment, where warmth, color, perfume, and the aural coolness of plashing water, all woo the senses at once.

Schoenemann found the door of the villa wide open like the gate. He stood on the threshold of a square hall, solemn and silent as a temple; and the Medicean Venus, who, from her pedestal of porphyry, was reflected at all her white and lovely length in the marble floor below, appeared like the goddess of the shrine. On either hand were doorways closed by heavy curtains, but there was no sight or sound of human life. Only the noise of water from a vase of roses overturned upon a sidetable, falling drop-wise into a self-formed pool on the pavement below. Only this, and the murmur of a bee, which had followed the young man in from the garden, broke the stillness. And when presently the water was all drained away, and the bee having found out the flowers settled down to enjoy them, the silence grew intense.

Emil told himself he had come upon a fairy

palace, of which the inhabitants had long ago been touched to sleep. He stood there upon the threshold, and savored a perfect enjoyment. He was not in the least embarrassed. The possessor of genius never is. He feels himself at all times and in all places far above external circumstances. Nature has crowned him king; and though a king may meet his equals, none stand above him. It is only the consciousness of a real or fancied inferiority that causes embarrassment.

For some little time the young man remained quiescent, because the beauty, silence, and solitude of his surroundings pleased him; but when presently he noticed a doorway of which the curtains were not closed, he thought it natural to walk straightway in.

He found himself in a large drawing-room, with a parqueted floor, an admirably painted ceiling, and walls hung with silk brocade. Three long windows looked out across the garden on to the Rhine, and a fourth window at the farther end of the room stood open on to a conservatory filled with tropical plants. There were flowers here too, and the stronger fragrance of tuberose and gardenia effaced the remembrance of the roses outside.

But the only object which appealed to Schoenemann's interest was a grand piano placed at an angle to this conservatory door. There are men who go into a room and leave it again, having seen absolutely nothing of its contents. Others there are who will give not only a correct inventory of all the furniture, but an appraisement of every article at its just price. There are those who see only the pictures, and those who see only the books; and some among the latter cannot resist taking a book up from the table or down from the shelf, although they knew their immediate expulsion were to be the consequence.

Schoenemann was affected in this way by musical instruments. He could not keep his fingers off them. Now he crossed over to the piano, opened it, and seated himself at the key-board with the same calmness and self-absorption as at the hired instrument in his Leipsic lodging, or at the wheezy old spinnet in the tiny living-room at home. He began to transmute back through his fingers, with the god-like faculty given to musicians alone, all the impressions of life, and joy, and beauty which his soul had received. At first with a certain hesitation, as his fingers sought the right chords — a hesitation still audible in the first eight bars, before comes the change of key — the harmonies rose and swelled and flooded the room with sound, until by that most unique and beautiful transition — I write with my eyes upon the published score — he passed to the light scherzo movement, which paints so well Nature's joyousness, and which yet, like Nature, to those who know her best, reveals an undersong of pain. Cruder, no doubt, in places than in its now perfected form, the work which has appealed to so many thousands of feeling hearts ever since, must have possessed an extraordinary fascination on the day when it was first drawn, warm and palpitating, out of silence by the power of the musician's soul.

The piano was placed so that the player faced the Rhine windows; and as Emil played, his gaze travelled across the river, and rested on the congregated roofs of his own village; but, rapt by the melodies he created, he was raised to an ideal world. He was unconscious of the instrument he played on, of the realities around him.

Velvet curtains hung on either side of the conservatory door, fell in voluminous folds, and lay on the floor in masses of drapery to delight a painter's heart. While Schoenemann played, one of these curtains was pulled gently aside, to reveal, hitherto concealed behind it, a very young girl. She had been sitting there reading, until the warmth of the day, the silence, and the enervating perfumes of the flowers had sent her to sleep. The book, a slim volume of Goethe's "Lieder," still lay open where it had slipped to her feet. If she had dreamed she was in heaven listening to the music of the spheres, she awoke to find the music was real; and she drew aside the curtain to perceive, with blue astonished eyes, a veritable flesh-and-blood young man, an entire stranger, seated at the piano before her.

Schoenemann struck the final chords, and slowly released the notes one by one. The faint harmonies still delighted his ear, when his glance fell upon the young girl. He looked at her, not with surprise, but with interest that passed into a passionate pleasure. In a flash of light he caught a resemblance between her and the ideal woman he had vainly sought since boyhood. The next moment, real and ideal were inextricably blended, and he devoted himself, body and soul, to the worship of Marie von Dittenheim. If his very first words did not tell her what had happened to him, at least his eyes must have done so; for, leaning on the piano and blushing deeply, she murmured in broken phrases her thanks for his music, and her praise, while her mind swung like a pendulum between terror and joy.

II.

THAT evening Emil sought out Harms, and overflowed to him on the subject of the Contesse Marie.

"She is the most beautiful creature I have ever met! Where were your eyes, Harms, not to have seen it? Wonderful man that you are! You have always spoken of her to me as a mere child. If I ever pictured her to myself at all, it was as a most ordinary young person. But she is holy as an angel, and exquisite as a Grecian statue into whom the gods have just breathed life. Just so must Galatea have looked when she stepped down from her pedestal to Pygmalion. Have you not noticed her throat? It is like marble, as white, as columnar, as softly rounded. You feel irresistibly inclined to lay your hand on its smooth contours, precisely as you desire to touch some subtly modelled piece of statuary."

Harms was bewildered, as much by Emil's warmth of language as by the new light his praises shed over the little Contesse. In point of fact, Harms had hitherto considered her as an amiable, nice-looking, but not unordinary young girl. Now, influenced as ever by Emil, he began to readjust this opinion. Certainly she had a full white throat — this was a point about her he remembered; but he had never felt tempted to touch it in the way Emil described. His attitude towards Woman was altogether too timorous to allow him to entertain any such poetic idea.

"And then her hair!" pursued Schoenemann; "I like that light-brown crinkly sort of hair. And it is gathered back into a loose knot behind, from which a golden haze escapes to float like an aureola about her face."

In true lover-fashion he saw beauties where the sane man might reasonably have found defects.

"She has no eyelashes, Harms, or scarcely any. Have you observed? But then her eyelids have curves that Phidias might have copied. And, after all, eyelashes are a type of low organization. Cattle and deer have them in far greater abundance than man; while the highest point of human beauty, as achieved by the Greeks, is entirely devoid of them. Yet who has ever felt the need of giving eyelashes to the Milean Venus? And, Harms, what heavenly dove's eyes! the bluest blue I have ever seen. There are no eyes like blue eyes, I think."

"Dark eyes are beautiful too," Harms answered. Emil's own were "black as our eyes endure;" but Harms was thinking of other eyes less beautiful than Emil's, but which he was once in the way of loving even better.

"Marie! Marie!" murmured the young man rapturously; "the name of Marie has acquired quite a new meaning for me. I am coming to consider it the most beautiful name in the world."

"It has always seemed so to me," said Harms, with a certain shyness; but Emil was too self-absorbed to remember that Harms had any particular reason for caring about the name.

"Yes?" he said carelessly; "but being my sister's name, it had become a household word to me, devoid of meaning. Now only, has its significance and its poetry returned. I am to

"THE ELEGIE."

go over to Bellavista again next Friday. Ah, how shall I live through the days and the nights till then."

The two men were walking in the woods above Klettendorf. They reached a point in the steep ascent where a clearing had been made, and a bench placed that the climber might rest awhile and enjoy the view. The trees fell away on either hand, permitting the eye to travel down over umbrageous masses of foliage to the river far below; to the level opposite shore, where stretched the gardens of Godesberg; to where beyond them a glowing sun sank down towards a horizon of distant trees. And as he sank, long ranks of crimson cloudlets radiated out and up to the very zenith of the sky, while the broad-bosomed Rhine flowing below was stained to a corresponding crimson glory.

Emil and Harms sat down on the bench, which was an old and favorite haunt of theirs. The younger man continued his love-litany. The elder listened, uttered the necessary responses, and, like many another worshipper who prays devoutly with the lips, allowed his thoughts to stray away to personal matters. It was impossible for him not to recall that, on just such an evening as this six years ago, he and Emil had sat together on that same bench, and their talk then as now had been of love, but with this difference — then Harms had been the lover, Emil the listener; and he had listened in absolute silence to August's unexpected and unpleasing confession — listened until he could endure it no longer, but had broken out into a passion of protestation and grief. He had thrown himself over there upon the ground and wept ragingly. Harms could still see the slight boyish figure shaken by sobs, and the black head low among the grasses, half hidden by nodding ferns.

Whence came these tears? Harms had foolishly slipped into love with Emil's sister. He had known Marie Schoenemann since he first came to Klettendorf. She had been his piano-pupil as well as Emil. He had seen her grow from a child to a shy and silent maiden, to a woman gay, hopeful, and kind. She could talk and jest now, as well as knit and sew; could wash her men-folk's shirts as well as cook their dinners. Harms admired all she did. He saw in her a heaven-sent wife. But he had never dared think practically of marrying her, until the unexpected offer of a fairly good post at Bremen made marriage a possibility instead of a dream. And then he had been stricken dumb by the manner in which Emil had received his confidence. He had looked at the prone figure before him, and been filled with perplexity and pain.

The storm had passed as suddenly as it had broken. Emil had sprung up pale and with flashing eyes, to demonstrate to Harms his colossal selfishness in desiring to take Marie away from her recently widowed mother, not to speak of the irreparable loss his friendship and daily companionship would be to Emil himself. The boy had spoken with singular lucidity and force. He was one of those gifted people who, the moment they have adopted an opinion, are able to impose it upon others by mere strength of will. Instantly they marshal forward such an array of weighty arguments that even opponents are forced to admit reason is on the other side. While Emil had spoken, poor Harms had sunk through every stage of humiliation and self-reproach. Nor had the boy spared him for this. When the iron glows hot and malleable is not the moment to give over striking.

"And Marie does not care for you," he had

said, "except as a friend. Of that I am certain. Who could have better opportunities of judging than I? To tell her of your feelings towards her would be to destroy forever the harmonious relations existing between you. She will marry, of course, some day; but it must be with a man more suited to her than you. Marie is twenty, but in many respects even younger than I am. You are nearly forty, and old for your years. What possible sympathy could there be between you?"

"There is something in what you say," August had admitted humbly; and he realized for the first time that youth was irrevocably gone. Such knowledge usually comes with a shock and an extraordinary bitterness. For so many years one has been young, very young, the youngest of one's company.

"There would, of course, be little inducement for a girl to leave her own people and begin life in a new place for my sake. It was folly of me ever to think of it. I will do so no more. But keep my secret, Emil, that I may keep her friendship. I would sooner see her and you daily, and be of some use to you both, than meet with all the good fortune in the world elsewhere."

In consequence of this conversation Harms had declined the Bremen offer, and from that day he strenuously endeavored to put from him all idle hopes. But to-night scene and circumstance brought back past dreams so vividly, he could not at once trample them under foot. For a while he lost himself in them, and the pains of renunciation were renewed. Whereby he came to sympathize all the more strongly with Emil, who appeared to him to be opening the first volume of an equally unpropitious love-story. For August found it impossible to contemplate seriously an alliance between a Dittenheim and the son of Franz Schoenemann. He thought he could gauge the Graefin's amazed reception of such an idea.

"Did you see no one beside Contesse Marie?" he asked Emil.

"A vague-looking lady with red eyebrows came in, but I did not observe her much."

"That would be the English governess," said Harms.

"And then I was summoned into another room to be presented to the Graefin."

"Ah, now! what did you think of her?" asked Harms, with interest. "Sad she should be so delicate, is it not? But she is still universally considered a very beautiful woman." He himself thought her, so far as appearance went, better worth praise than her little daughter.

"Perhaps," said Emil, briefly; "I scarcely remember. Do you know, Harms," he went on, clasping his two hands behind his neck with an action which was habitual to him, "I have made a discovery: all life and all art is but a preparation for Love. Love is the end of life, and I do not seem to have really lived until to-day. I have eaten and drunk, have slept and have awakened, but, like an infant on its nurse's arm, have hitherto been utterly unconscious of the real meaning and purpose of existence. In the same way my music has been but a vague groping after joys and beauties which have forever eluded me. I have played on an instrument from which the key-note has been missing, and the result has been as unsatisfying as a series of unresolved chords. But henceforth all will be different. With Marie as my sweetheart and wife, I shall scale the highest pinnacles."

Harms was staggered by this confidence.

"But," objected he, "do you think the Dittenheims would ever consent to accept you as a suitor?"

"Why not?" asked Emil, superbly. "Love makes all things equal; and if she loves me, she is raised to the same level as mine."

Harms stared, doubting whether his ears did not betray him.

"Or is it possible you mean she is what fools call 'well-born,' and I am not? To my mind the best born is he who has received the gifts of the gods direct. Read Plato. Does he not put musicians highest of all — even above poets and orators? False modesty shall never lead me to deny or belittle a possession which I prize and honor a thousand times more than life."

"Yes, yes, I agree with all you say," cried Harms; "and those whose opinion is better worth having than mine to-day put genius above birth. But will the Dittenheims do so? I cannot endure to see you preparing for yourself such bitter disappointment."

"I love this girl," said Emil; "and if she loves me — and she will love me — no power on earth shall stand between us. I have set my whole heart and mind on this thing, and you or the Dittenheims could as easily turn me from it as you could make the Rhine there flow backwards."

From childhood up, Emil had achieved his own way — hitherto in silence. This was the first occasion on which he openly announced his intention of always achieving it.

The upper rim of the sun-ball now touched the trees behind the gardens of Godesberg. Looking down on the river, the two men saw it all orange and indigo, while the sky flamed with orange and rose. They began their descent through the twilight of the woods. When they gained the open hillside, the heavens were painted with the softer colors of the afterglow. In the east, river and sky were red with reflected light; but in the west, sky and river were of an exquisite unearthly green. The islands and wooded promontories rose up with a new sombreness, and to Emil's fancy the trees justled closer together and moved into new combinations as he watched them through the gathering gloom.

III.

SCHOENEMANN, who would recognize no difficulties in the way of his love for Marie von Dittenheim, chose to observe no reticences either. Before Friday came, his whole family, I had almost said all Klettendorf, knew of his passion. Precisely as he had overflowed on the subject to Harms, so he overflowed to his mother, his aunt Kunie, his sister Marie. The two elder women were dismayed. The discipline of life had taught them to place expediency before sentiment. Besides, Emil's sentiments appeared to them exaggerated, his hopes impossible to fulfil. But although, when alone together, they reiterated the insuperable difficulties which barred his wishes, neither ventured to point these out to the young man himself. Their love for him was largely tempered with fear.

Marie Schoenemann, on the contrary, was strangely stirred by the event. Here, for the first time in her life, was a real love-story beginning under her very eyes. She could not hear enough of it from Emil; nor could she recover from her surprise that the Contesse Marie, whom she had last seen two summers ago, a little girl in short frocks, with plaited hair down her back, should be capable of inspiring such a passion as her brother's.

But, besides elation, she was conscious of feeling a species of envy, and when at night, combing out her long dark hair, she looked in the glass at her agreeable reflection, she longed for some such happiness as Marie von Dittenheim's to befall herself. She was already six-and-twenty; it was time the lover came. And now, while she cooked and scoured, washed Emil's shirts and ironed them, she ceased to sing. For the first time in her life her youthful confidence in her own future began to be shaken.

Emil, who did not lean on chance, but had the lofty assurance his future should be as he chose to make it, lost neither time nor opportunity in furthering his desires. His second interview with the little Contesse was decisive. I know not how he managed to again escape the company of the vague lady with the fiery eyebrows. I only know that determined lovers always do succeed in managing such things. But he did not leave Bellavista a second time without having won from the young girl her tremulous admission that she loved him too. Masculine fire such as his could not burn without awakening a corresponding glow in the feminine mirror.

The lady with the eyebrows, though constantly out-generalled by Emil in matters of detail, could not be altogether blinded to the state of affairs. She carried her surmises to the Graefin, who, first incredulous, then disdainfully amused, caused a letter to be written to Emil putting a stop to her daughter's lessons. Emil continued to visit Bellavista as a friend. The servants had orders to deny him the door. Aided at every point by the little Contesse herself, he contrived to meet her in the Rhine garden. The Graefin, now angry in earnest, kept the girl a prisoner in the house. Emil wrote her letters, which were confiscated before reaching her. He determined to make a bold appeal to the Graf to sanction a betrothal. The Graefin appealed to her husband on the same day for his interference and support.

Dittenheim turned from a perusal of Schoenemann's extraordinary epistle to listen to his wife's denunciation of the writer. He sent for his daughter, and drew from her a meagre confession and an abundance of tears. Alone again in his study, he gave himself up to a sense of dispassionate entertainment. He was a student of human nature, and constantly deplored the fact that conformity and mental flabbiness rendered so few humans profitable studies. But he scented in Emil's letter a refreshing amount of originality of mind. It was undeniably original that the son of his deceased under-ranger should write and calmly demand the hand of his only daughter in marriage. He must see between four walls what manner of man it was who could prefer so audacious a request.

Emil accordingly came over again to Bellavista at Graf Dittenheim's desire, who, devoting eye and ear to the young man before him, told himself he had not for months past experienced so keen a pleasure. And indeed there are no pleasures comparable to those of observation. To these alone time bringeth not satiety, and the most inveterate sportsman rejoices less when his prey falls living into his hands than does the character-hunter on first turning a fresh page in the history of his fellows.

"You tell me my daughter is as much in love with you as you are with her? Good. Love makes all things equal, you say? Good again. You won't take a seat? Very good; very good. Continue walking up and down if it gives you any solace."

Emil for the first time in his life was slightly disconcerted. He had thought to experience the most violent opposition, — scorn, perhaps vituperation. He had armed himself with counter-scorn, with passion, eloquence, irresistible pleadings to beat it down; and he found the expected foe very courteous, very bland, almost cordial. It was like going out to assault a castle, and finding yourself engulfed instead in a smooth, smiling, and treacherous sea.

Dittenheim, leaning comfortably back in an easy-chair, noted Emil's every look, registered his smallest word, and while he appeared to be merely listening, was collating evidence, weighing it, passing judgment. Not for one moment did he contemplate an alliance between his daughter and his late servant's son; but he fancied he detected in Emil's own character that which would have made him refuse the honor, no matter how highly born the young man had been.

The Graf, pointing the ends of his moustache with white fingers, smiled up at him. "You are aware," he went on, "that the Contesse and you belong to widely different ranks? Yes, yes, you have told me already that genius is superior to birth; that such gifts as yours received straight from the gods are better than a worn-out name, handed down through a line of enfeebled progenitors. No doubt you are right. Only there is this point to be considered. Any fool can verify the social value of a name; but as to the genius, the supposed possessor, when young and unknown as you are, stands in the position of a page who has still to win his spurs. The genius is unproven. You say you can prove it? Very good indeed. Go out into the world, make your reputation there, come back in seven years' time — and then I will reconsider the question of giving you my daughter."

Emil protested against seven years. It was a lifetime.

"But can you reach the goal in less? You know the difficulties of the career you have chosen. Besides, did ever man yet make a reputation worth having before he was thirty? Putting the Contesse out of the question, are seven years too long for the work you have mapped yourself out?"

"Give me ten years," said Emil, impetuously, "and I reach the top of the ladder."

"And I as a reasonable man offer to take you while you are yet a few rungs lower down. Only, that I should see you first fairly mounted, is not, I think, too much to ask. Go out into

"THE ELEGIE." 41

the world, go to Paris," — there was, in fact, a project that Schoenemann should go to Paris to complete his studies; Brockhoff, his Leipsic master, had recommended it; it had been a question of ways and means which had hitherto prevented him from acting on Brockhoff's advice, — "study, succeed, set the name of Schoenemann as high in the musical world as Dittenheim stands in society circles, come back in seven years crowned with laurels, and Marie is yours — provided of course she still wishes it."

Emil required at the least a formal betrothal, but this the Graf pleasantly refused. "With seven years' separation before you it is better both should be absolutely free. But why let that depress you? What are words or promises? How can they make more binding an affection which you tell me nothing can weaken or change? Betrothals may be useful between persons who believe more in the sanctity of a promise than in the sanctity of love; but to you, and presumably to my daughter, who understand so perfectly love's divine, unalterable nature, it could only be a work of supererogation."

"But," the young man objected, "you and

all her people will endeavor to make her forget me?"

"I shall certainly try," admitted Dittenheim. "I should be very glad to think I could succeed. Unfortunately, Marie is of a steadfast disposition." He looked at his visitor smilingly, had a phrase on the tip of his tongue, bit it back as imprudent, and, after all, could not resist letting it go. "It is rather on your inconstancy that I build my hopes!"

Emil was indignant, demanded explanations, and received them after this fashion:—

"Marie is a good but ordinary girl; you are an exceptional young man. It is not probable she will ever again be wooed with such poetic fire and passion. She will compare future suitors with you to their disadvantage. The mere fact of your absence will not efface your memory from her heart. I even contemplate the possibility of her remaining intolerably true. She will continue to lead a sheltered and more or less monotonous life, running always in accustomed grooves. It will be difficult to obliterate the impression you have created. Besides which, she has reached the highest point of her development. She will never be much other than what she now is.

But you have still a long way to go. It is safe to predict that five years hence will find you a very different person from what you are to-day. You will have discovered new wants, of which at the present moment you have no suspicion. You will have rid yourself of many old possessions, which have their uses while we linger in the valley, but become impedimenta when climbing the mountain-side. And then you will have met in Paris the most refined, the most charming, the most intellectual women in the world. I have lived there, and speak with knowledge. You will look back with astonishment at this *grande passion* of yours, this green love-episode, and you will remember, with gratitude let me hope, that you are absolutely free. This at least, my young friend, is what I reckon on, and it partly explains the equanimity with which I have listened to your entirely preposterous proposals."

The frankly cynical speech was delivered with a confidence which Emil found extremely galling. The well-chosen words fell like drops of ice-water upon his red-hot passion. They left a rankling wound long in his breast. He could not forget Dittenheim's looks and tones, which asserted a superiority in worldly wisdom hard to forgive. An immense desire to prove the Graf wrong laid hold of Emil, who said to himself that even in the impossible case of his ever loving Marie less than at that moment, he would marry her merely to show Graf Dittenheim how much he had been mistaken.

Meanwhile Emil's departure for Paris became a settled thing, and his arrangements were facilitated, unknown to himself, by Dittenheim's liberality towards his mother. The Graf fully believed in the wisdom of building a golden bridge for the retreating foe.

Emil asked for a final interview with his little sweetheart; and because the girl kissed her father's hand, and wept over it, and besought ardently for the same favor, Dittenheim permitted it. He laughed at himself for doing so, and told his wife he was weak-minded to be moved by a woman's tears. And she, turning on him incensed and sunken eyes, from the sofa she could now no longer leave, declared he was worse than weak-minded, he was criminal. "The whole of life is only a play to you," she said, "and even your own daughter but one of the players. You would not mind what shameful part she took, so long as you from your box could see and hear comfortably all that was done and said." Which, however, was not altogether true.

All the same, the interview took place one August evening, in the Rhine garden of Bellavista. Here a terrace of stone overhangs the river. Here it is good to walk and watch the waters flowing down from the Sieben Gebirge towards the broad plains of Koeln. Here, leaning on the stone balustrade, Schoenemann held Marie's plump little red hand between his own nervous white ones, and implored her over and over again to be true.

"I think it is you who will first forget me!" she told him, for she too had heard of the sirens of Paris.

"Never shall I cease remembering you! Alone, in exile, among strangers, how could I forget? But you will meet some man of your own rank, and your people will persuade you into taking him."

"Ah, indeed I would die sooner!" she declared, with the pardonable exaggeration of the very young.

Emil had bought in Bonn two crystal lockets exactly alike, — cheap enough trinkets, but as dear as his purse could afford; painfully ugly but safe guardians for their destined locks of hair. The lovers exchanged these mementos with due ceremony. They were to be worn day and night as talismans against misfortunes, and pledges of secretly plighted troth. Marie slipped his on to her little gold neck-chain, which she had worn with an Immaculate Conception medal since childhood, and gave him these also. He tied hers with a ribbon round her throat, and hid the locket in the bosom of her dress. And finally, after an incredibly protracted leave-taking, and manifold signs of impatience from the red-eyebrowed lady who played propriety at a little distance off, the young people parted with vows, tears, kisses, and mutual heart-break.

IV.

Emil's first months in Paris, his solitariness, the difficuties he encountered, and the extent to which he enhanced these by his own proud and impetuous bearing, may be found in the biographies. I leave all this aside, being concerned in following one thread only of his story, in casting light on a single episode in a career which boasted many episodes, and which, dating from his arrival in Paris, embraced wider and more varied interests daily.

By the time that he had published the first book of "Preludes," the worst struggle was over. He was beginning to be favorably noticed. Custom had softened his early detestation of the city and its ways into tolerance, which in its turn grew imperceptibly into affection. As in the beginning he had wondered how he could ever endure the new life and strange people, so at length he asked himself how he could ever again exchange the intellectual brilliancy of Paris for the somnolence of a German town.

At first the idea of Marie von Dittenheim had been his constant companion. But as his days grew more busy, he could only remember her in leisure moments, and by and by when he occasionally recalled her image, it was to reproach himself with having so habitually forgotten it. For he was now beginning to make that long succession of warm friendships which is one of the remarkable features of his life; and to the friend of the hour he was always passionately and exclusively attached. It is true, these intimacies were seldom of long duration, and yet it was not fickleness which brought them to a close. The moment that Schoenemann discovered that he had passed his friend intellectually, he deliberately threw him aside. He said, and with some show of reason, that friendship being an exchange of mutual benefit, directly one ceases to derive advantage from one's friend, the friendship by that very reason is dissolved.

The most durable of his friendships was that with Madame Vasseur, some account of whom is pertinent to my sketch, since it was perhaps as much because of the empire which this lady began to exercise over him, as from any other cause, that he eventually held true to his German sweetheart.

Flore Vasseur would be now entirely forgotten but for her connection with Schoenemann (which led to her tragic death in Rome some years later), on which account a brief notice is given of her by most of his biographers. She was, however, in her day, a flower-painter of some repute. Curiously enough, I recently came across one of her studies in an *appartement garni* of the Quartier Marais. It was a fruit-piece splashily painted, but all its colors faded to a uniform neutrality of tint. Nothing remained of its pristine glories, save the "Flore" boldly written in vermilion letters across one corner, and the date, "1842," underneath. She voluntarily sacrificed future glory for the praise of her contemporaries, and obtained by illegitimate methods a brilliancy of coloring as unrivalled as it was transitory. When it was pointed out to her that her work would not endure, she replied it would probably endure quite as long as it deserved to do. She had not the smallest desire it should be immortal.

"I wish to leave room for those who come after me," said she, jesting; "and every twenty years will produce a flower-painter as good or better than I. Such talent as mine is perennial as the flowers themselves. It is not like the genius of Emil Schoenemann. The true musician and the aloe-blossom appear only once in a century."

Madame Vasseur lived just outside Paris, at Cerçay-sous-Senart. Her acquaintance with Emil dated from the third year of his Paris sojourn. They were introduced to each other at a musical evening given by the Pleyels. Emil had by this time just made the discovery that general society was distasteful to him, that the adulation people now gave him was worse than their former neglect, and that the round of so-called amusement which he had at first followed with youthful ardor was in reality as insipid as it was enervating.

Madame Vasseur attracted him from the first moment he met her. She was not so pretty as many women, but she was vivacious, intelligent, and extraordinarily sympathetic. He acquired the habit of spending a good deal of his time at Cerçay. He found he could work there under happier conditions than in Paris. After an industrious and solitary morning, he liked to spend the rest of the day in Flore's studio. Here, to please him, she had placed a grand piano, on which he would try over his latest compositions, while she painted with rapid, skilful hand. Or if he wished to talk, she put down her brushes and gave him her whole attention. She had pieced together the scraps he had let fall of his early history, and took so vivid an interest in all that concerned him that she could speak of the incidents of his boyhood, and of the people of Klettendorf, with almost as much confidence as though personally acquainted with them. She knew, too, all about the Contesse Marie; but on this subject at least, it must be confessed, her attitude was slightly chilling.

When she first knew Emil, four years of freedom still lay before him; an eternity, he told himself; for the years ahead always seem vague and long as centuries; it is only when one looks back upon them that one sees they have gone like so many days. And in the beginning of their friendship, his infrequent references to the young girl troubled Flore but little; a thousand things might yet happen to release him from a position she felt sure no longer held for him any charm. But when, at last, he began to speak of his departure for Germany as likely to take place within a year — within a few months — her feeling towards Mademoiselle von Dittenheim deepened into dislike. It was characteristic of Schoenemann that, seeing this, he should refer to the subject more often than he might otherwise have done, and that he should adopt a tone of decision he was in reality far from feeling.

For he began to consider every day more seriously whether it was not a piece of quixotic folly to remain bound to a woman whom he had long ago recognized as unessential to his scheme of life. His mind swayed this way and that. Whenever he received a letter from Harms, he became for the next few weeks quite determined neither to return to Germany nor to fulfil his engagement; for poor August's expressed or implied confidence he would do both produced an entirely opposite effect to that which the writer intended. But Emil could not forget his interview with Graf Dittenheim. He would recall the man's shrewd amused eyes, hear again the complacent superiority of his tone, and again be filled with the strong determination to prove his suspicions had been baseless. And, naturally, there were many other motives pressing down the scale on this side or that. In real life conduct is ever complex; it is only in the story-books that we find it determined by a beautiful singleness of purpose. Thus, much as Schoenemann might believe he despised social rank, he could not be a German and not appreciate the honor of an alliance with a Dittenheim; and, however coldly egotistic he had become, he could not, as a man, stifle all feeling for the young girl, who, as Harms and rumor told him, still loved him so devotedly. Yet he knew that never again could she be anything but a burden to him; he knew he had passed her immeasurably, and that all the stimulus he found in such companionship as Flore's would be entirely wanting in his home life should he make Marie his wife. The problem how to act best was a knotty one.

He sat one evening in the studio, with a letter from Harms in his pocket, received that day. It was a more annoying letter than usual; for whereas Harms as a rule spoke of Emil's return as a matter of course, he now, to the young man's great surprise, urged him vehemently to return at once. "Do not wait for the summer, best of friends," wrote Harms, "but come immediately and claim your betrothed;" and then he hinted at some appalling misfortune overhanging the head of the little Contesse in dark enigmatical language, which aroused Emil's anger rather than his sympathy. He sat lost in thought, with set lips and a frown on his handsome forehead, while Madame Vasseur watched him pensively.

"What is the matter with you?" she asked him when the silence had endured some little time; "you are not happy to-night. Tell me what is troubling you."

"Do you think confession would make me happier?" said the young man, and his calm glances rested on her face with immense inward satisfaction. She had what he called such *fragende Augen*, eyes that seemed to ask and confide so much more than the smiling lips would confess to.

"Assuredly. I always find that to confess my troubles is the first step towards dismissing them."

"Because probably your troubles are not real ones. I do not see how a real trouble or perplexity is to be vanquished by imparting it to another mind — especially to a mind less capable of sustaining it."

"A flattering truth!" said Flore, laughing; and he found her childlike type of face delicious when she laughed. "But tell me, do you make no account of sympathy?"

"Not much. I begin to think that sympathy, like charity, is more harmful than helpful to the recipient."

"You are becoming so self-sufficing that I should advise you to imitate St. Simeon Stylites; build yourself a pillar, and make music on the top of it."

"It appears to me," said Emil, musing, "that as we advance — mentally — we do live, so to speak, each of us on the top of a pillar, and have less and less communication with our fellow-men. In childhood the love and praise of our home circle alone is essential to us; later on, we seek eagerly the wider appreciation of the world; but finally, we outgrow the necessity for either, and ask for nothing but the approbation of our own souls."

Flore, with her graceful head on one side, watched him smilingly. "You have not reached the highest point yet then," said she; "for you do not seem to-night entirely convinced of your soul's approbation. And I am glad of it," she added; "for when that time comes my poor praises will no longer give you any pleasure."

"Every man of course likes praise," said Emil; "but it is just as well to learn to do without it. I foresee little enough in the life that lies before me. That is to say, little intelligent praise; and none other is worth the having."

"Are you thinking of your German *fiancée?*" asked Flore.

"Yes; of my *fiancée* who is soon to be my wife."

She looked at him in silence, but still smiled. "You are determined to go in the summer?" she said presently.

"Even sooner. In fact I have received news

from home which seems to necessitate my immediate departure. I must return to Paris to-morrow to settle my affairs, and so to-night I have come to bid you good-by."

The sudden color that rose to her cheek, her momentary hesitation, did not pass unobserved by Schoenemann; but when she spoke, the gayety of her tone once more perplexed him.

"A most dramatic announcement!" she cried, "although I suspect the decision was only this moment come to. Well, you would have my best wishes were you going away for any other cause than that of your marriage; but I should be a poor friend indeed were I to affect to regard such a step as beneficial to you."

"Ah! I know your objections to marriage," said Emil; "although, coming from a married woman, the advice rings rather oddly."

"Oh, I! what does it matter about me? Whether I make more or less progress, am more or less happy, what difference does it make? But for the true artist, the man of genius, it is otherwise. The world asks from him, and rightly, the best he can give; and for the production of his best, happiness is an essential. How can he possibly be happy married to a woman with whom he has no sympathy?"

"True, undoubtedly," said Emil; "yet what can I do? Morally I am bound to keep my word. Besides, the girl loves me. Her happiness counts for something in the affair."

"She does not love you," cried Flore, "if she cannot sacrifice her happiness to her love. Why, I . . . that is to say, a woman who really loved a man would cheerfully see him married to another if it were for his greater good. But when she saw him going blindly to his own destruction, she would let the whole world perish, if by doing so she could save him."

"It is curious," said Schoenemann, speaking more to himself than his companion, "how one's opinions change. Seven years ago it seemed to me that life held nothing more desirable than my little sweetheart. Then I would have married her joyfully, and should have considered myself the most fortunate fellow in the world." He mused, clasping his hands behind his head with the action Flore knew so well. "Then I looked upon the whole of life merely as a preparation for love. Then it seemed to me that music itself was but a means of honoring the beloved one. Now I know that life and love too are but steps upward towards the attainment of the highest art, and the passion which seemed so beautiful in youth is only valuable for the deeper and wider emotions it enables us to express."

Madame Vasseur watched him with an indefinable air. "So you have outgrown love," she said, "as you have outgrown society, and as you will presently, no doubt, outgrow friendship. You progress so fast that with the best intentions in the world you could not promise to remain to-morrow where you stand to-day. Do you not see that for you it is madness to contemplate matrimony?"

"True again," he answered; "to give up in any measure my liberty and independence is to deduct just so much from the likelihood of producing good work. Yet it seems to me that, if Mademoiselle von Dittenheim still desires it, I am bound in honor to fulfil my engagement."

Flore's smile condensed a vast number of meanings. "What, have you not outgrown such puerile notions of honor also?" she cried.

"In point of fact," said Emil, seriously, "I begin to think I have. The honorableness of holding to the letter of a promise, when the spirit which quickened it is dead or changed, does seem sufficiently puerile. And yet —"

He found it most difficult to decide what to do. He remembered the satisfaction his infidelity would afford Graf Dittenheim, and he inclined to go; but he remembered also the urgency of Harms's entreaties that he should return home, and he was almost fixed in his determination to stay.

Madame Vasseur, who openly watched him, seemed to read his thoughts. A flash of triumph lighted her soft eyes. The pleasure she felt was too strong to be concealed, and she betrayed it in her smile, in her dimples, in the animation of her voice.

"You will not go!" she cried gayly. "Ah! I felt sure all along you could not go. And I confess the studio would seem a strange and desolate land without you. I have the fancy I could no longer paint if you were no longer here to play to me."

Schoenemann looked down the long and lofty room, with its half-lighted distances, its widely dispersed lamps, and said to himself he too should feel strange, rooted out from a life that had grown so congenial to him. Here at the piano he had spent delicious hours, weaving musical fancies into which all his surroundings made subtle entrance, — the blossoms, flowers, and creepers which during more than half the year trailed their lengths, shed their perfume, and spread their beauty all over the place; those other flowers scarcely less brilliant, which still during the winter months bloomed from the walls; the bizarre properties, the gorgeous bits of drapery, the thousand and one knick-knacks, every fold and piece of which he knew so well; Madame Vasseur's light graceful figure, and the small brown head held flower-fashion, now this side and now that, as she walked to and fro before her easel.

Yes, he recognized it was Flore herself whom he would miss most of all. She had acquired an influence over him which might in time grow irresistible. And as he glanced at her and listened to her confident assertions, he told himself she would use every means to increase and rivet her power. He felt she would make far greater claims on him than a Marie von Dittenheim could do. Here, even more than in marriage, was he likely to lose the independence he held so dear. Were he at the end of his life, he might perhaps be ready to acquiesce in this woman's gentle yoke; but now, in the zenith of his youth, with so much still to learn and to achieve, he must break it while he could yet do so without much pain.

As his hesitations finally condensed themselves into settled purpose, his brow cleared. Flore divined his intentions in the bright coldness of his glance. Her face lost its smile, and she sat in pale suspense.

"It is getting late," said he, rising, "and I have a great deal to do, so you must allow me to say good-night. Good-night and good-by both together. For at last I have made up my mind. I return to Germany after all."

V.

THE Dittenheims, father and daughter, were residing in Berlin. The Graefin had been laid to rest long since in the cemetery at Nice, the town wherein so many European health-seekers find only a grave.

Schoenemann did not purpose going straight to the capital. He broke his journey at Koeln, in order to spend half a week at Klettendorf. He desired particularly to see Harms, that he might reproach him for the irritating urgency of his letter. He intended to recapitulate to him all Flore's arguments against marriage, to prove incontestably that for him, Emil, it would be especially fatal; then, having reduced the unfortunate Harms to a state of abject despair, to go to move heaven and earth to make that marriage an accomplished fact. Quite at the back of his mind he rejoiced in the idea that, when all his predicted misery should have actually come to pass, he would be able to inflict on Harms a still more poignant regret.

Outside of these intentions he found a real pleasure in returning to Klettendorf. He wanted to see the village, the old home, his own people again. He loved them all because of the relation in which they stood to himself. He remembered with the greatest affection the little Emil of long ago; the boy who had run so light-heartedly up and down the highways of Klettendorf, or in the dark cottage room had sat so many hours at the loose-tongued old piano, trying to reproduce the song of the birds, or the gush and babble of the mountain streams. From the beginning all the world had made music to him; it was to beautiful and harmonious sounds his affections had first responded. Almost a baby, he had heard melodies in the winter winds which torment the woods above Klettendorf, and the Rhine forever flowing swiftly seawards had taught him harmonies.

He remembered now, as though it were yesterday, numberless incidents which had impressed themselves on his child's mind, in which either his dead father or mother, Marie or Harms, arose as attendant figures; the humble house, the poor village, as familiar background.

There was a unique occasion on which he had come into collision with his father, who had reprimanded him with some roughness. For two hours afterwards he had lain upon the floor, weeping tropically, and refusing to be comforted. He was about five years old then, and he had said to his mother in reference to the event a few days later, "I am always happy, and I wanted to be unhappy to see what it was like."

The man Emil smiled as he looked back on the child's curiosity to probe sensations, — a curiosity which, on another occasion, had made him persist, despite of gathering nausea, in assisting at the slaughter of a pig. He had stood a stubborn and white-faced spectator of the scene, until he had fallen down on the stones in a faint. But the smoking blood, the shrieks of the victim, had worked upon his mind, and he had composed a little battle-song for piano and fiddle to commemorate the impression. He had tried to represent horror and tumultuous movement, and to simulate by long wailing notes on the violin the cries of the dying. He wondered what had become of this early *opus*, which Harms had praised enthusiastically, as, by the way, he had praised every single work Schoenemann had produced since.

He remembered how as a child he had adored his mother; how she had once seemed to him not only the most beautiful and the kindest of women, but the cleverest also. It was only very gradually he came to discover her wanting in perceptions, and too occupied in mending and cooking to have time to listen to his music. By the age of ten he had already begun to lean more on his sister Marie, who was then seventeen, and full of the hopes, the gayety, the carelessness of a young girl. Marie was devoted to the clever little brother, and no sacrifice was too much for her to make him. When he wanted her company she would give up any personal pleasure, or rise at four to get through the household tasks, so as to be free for his service. He remembered the hours he had spent with her dreaming aloud, while

"THE ELEGIE." 65

she listened and praised. And then, as he came to be fifteen, she was less necessary to him than Harms; he had learned all she was able to teach him; she was as a book he had read through, and one of those books that do not bear reading twice. Henceforth all his spare time was spent in August's room, discussing life, music, glory; improvising on his piano, or climbing with him the wooded hills that shelter Klettendorf, walking through the apple and cherry orchards that gather round it. At that time he simply could not have existed in his narrow village but for the sympathy and affection he found in Harms. No wonder he had opposed August's desire to marry his sister; and Marie herself had become dear to him as ever, the moment there had seemed a possibility of losing her. But as it turned out, they might have married, so far as he was concerned; and he thought with a faint and natural contempt of the weakness of poor Harms in allowing the whole course of his life to be altered by the will of a boy.

Memories such as these beguiled the way to Klettendorf; and for himself he was filled with a tender compassion. What a foolish affectionate fellow he had been. Ever ready to expend his heart on other people, ever believing he had found in each new personality the brother soul which was to satisfy him, ever condemned to struggle upwards alone. His past was strewn with the friendships he had tried in the balance and found wanting.

He was already beginning to gauge the limits of Harms's capacities when he had met the Contesse Marie. His passion for her had been but transitory, yet how beautiful while it lasted. She would always retain a certain interest for him, in having been the passive object which had awakened those heavenly feelings of first love. But he had long seen clearly that it was the light of his own genius which had transfigured her, and that he had fallen at the feet of an idol of his own creation. Ah, the wild, the wonderful, the delicious generosity of youth! He could not restrain a smile when he reflected, that in those days he had desired to consecrate his whole powers, his whole future life, to the service of a little moon-faced girl with round eyes and red hands.

He supposed her hands were no longer red. Harms had written she was grown thin, and had otherwise much changed. But the real Marie must of course remain the same, a soul on a lower plane, which could never be raised to his, any more than he could successfully stoop to hers. And such was to be their union, one in name but never in fact.

He could and would show her kindness, bear himself with patience, but henceforth all his highest desires and sympathies must be unshared. Mournful anticipations of the future had begun to blot out the pleasanter reminiscences of the past when he reached Klettendorf and stood with his hand on the familiar garden gate.

The click of the latch brought two women out from the cottage to greet him: an old woman with bands of yellow-white hair showing in front of a close net cap, — his Aunt Kunie; and a woman no longer young, with the expression women acquire whose lives have been all duty without one satisfying joy, — this was the once bright and hopeful sister.

Schoenemann sat down with them to the meal they had prepared for him; the best they could manage, and yet almost barbarous in its homely ingredients and rude cooking, after the civilizations of Paris. The coarse table-cloth was distasteful to him, so were the horn-handled knives and forks, the earthen beer-mugs with their pewter tops. Aunt Kunie produced in his honor the Bowle wine, which she made herself from elder-flowers and oranges, and which as a boy he had thought so delicious. Now he found it detestable, and could scarcely bring himself to finish the small glassful she ladled out for him. Her hesitating, trivial conversation teased him; he was only annoyed by her well-meant efforts to please. She thought herself bound to talk about Paris, the friends he had made there, and the musical world. It cost him a struggle to reply to her with civility.

When he looked at Marie, he was amazed to see how plain and old she had become. Again the thought crossed his mind it might have been better for her had Harms made her his wife. Certainly no man would marry her now.

He almost wished he had never returned to Klettendorf at all. His memory-pictures would have remained entirely agreeable had he never confronted them with the reality. However, he had been obliged to come in order to see Harms.

"What is all this about the Dittenheims?" he asked his sister. "August writes such mys-

"THE ELEGIE." 69

terious letters. Marie von Dittenheim has lived well enough without me for seven years. What is the 'urgent need' she has for me now?"

"People say she has always counted on your coming," said the other Marie.

"Well, and have I not come? I always intended coming this summer, but it would have been more convenient to have come a few months later on. Only August, finally, gave me no peace. Where is he? Why is he not here to meet me?"

"He will be here at four. He had a lesson to give across the river."

"Just the same life, I suppose? He still lodges with Schumacher?"

"Just the same," said the sister, drily; "no change but one ever comes to the poor."

"You will wish to go and visit your blessed mother's grave?" said Aunt Kunie. "Marie will take you there, and you will be back in time for coffee."

Emil walked with his sister to the quiet God's acre on the hill. He stood before the slate headstone inscribed to the memory of Franz Schoenemann and Marie Bleibtren his wife, and thought over many things. It is certain that a man cannot stand by the grave of his

"THE ELEGIE."

mother and not experience emotion. He had told her once, in a transport of child affection, that when he was a man he would never leave her, but would live with her always. And yet he had not found it possible to get to her dying bed. He wished now it had been possible; but it had not been so, although he had forgotten by this time the particular obstacles which had prevented him. He left the graveyard trying to recall them. He walked fast, absorbed in thought, and his sister was left far behind.

A man in slovenly clothes stood by Aunt Kunie in the little garden watching for his return. Emil saw it was Harms, and said to himself he too had changed for the worse. He looked broken-down, blunted, unsatisfied with life, yet hopeless of mending it. After kissing Emil with his old affection, he waited for Marie to come up, and exchanged a few words with her of the most ordinary commonplace. The hopes he had once entertained were long ago extinguished. Now he was so wedded to the dull routine of life, he would have dreaded any change. He had reached the point where all divinely implanted discontent withers away, and could meet the woman he had once loved,

"THE ELEGIE." 71

and no color rise to his cheek, his heart beat no whit the faster.

Her lot was perhaps harder still; she had never known the happiness of even unrequited love, but had lost youth and freshness, youth's adjuncts of hope and high spirits, and the gayety that lends a passing charm to glance and smile, nursing in secret the agonizing conviction that never once to any man had she afforded eye-satisfaction or heart-pleasure. She treated Harms with a certain bitterness, but there was no particular meaning in this; it was her attitude towards all the world.

Aunt Kunie had prepared coffee for two in the parlor. She and Marie retired to drink theirs in the kitchen, knowing that Emil would prefer being left alone with his friend. Harms sat for long silent and embarrassed. Momentarily he grew more impressed with Emil's immense superiority, visible even in such trifles as his dress, his manners, the way in which he held his head. He saw that any equality or companionship with his former pupil and friend was now out of the question. He feared he had shown presumption in the warmth of his greetings. Emil was obliged to question him before he regained courage to talk.

"The Contesse Marie is ill? Is that the misfortune you hint at? You seem to imply she is dying of love for me. The idea is absurd. Now and again I have heard of the Dittenheims from Berliners in Paris, and from all accounts my betrothed has become a most accomplished young lady of the world, — the exact counterpart of her mother."

"You still love her, my poor Emil?" asked Harms, earnestly.

"Does it not look like it," parried the other, "since I am here?"

"You wish to make her your wife?"

"I mean, of course, to make her my wife."

"I knew it; I could trust you!" cried Harms, enthusiastically. "I knew that you, a Rhinelander, would be true. And she, I am sure, loves you still; but she is naturally weak, and then reports reached her — she spoke of them to me last year — and of course her family made the most of them. But you can save her yet. Go at once to Berlin; present yourself. It is fixed for next week, I believe; but when she sees you she will retract her word. With you beside her she will feel herself strong enough to face the consequences, and you will rescue her from the worst possible fate. All the world knows what that man's character is; and besides, how could he ever satisfy a woman who has been honored with such an affection as yours?"

Schoenemann stared at the speaker with a glacial irritation. "You are raving," said he; "I have no conception of your meaning. Speak German, — if you are able, — and tell me what fate threatens my betrothed."

"Then command yourself, Emil," said the good Harms, himself greatly agitated; "keep calm, I implore you! She has yielded at last to over-persuasion, and has consented to marry her cousin, Baron Max. The wedding is arranged for Friday next."

VI.

Harms's words surprised Emil as much as a douche of cold water in the face. He sat silent. Then he experienced a movement of sensible relief. He saw for the first time in all its completeness how dear to him was the liberty with which he had been prepared to part. He was free, and in the only way possible to him, through the initiative of Marie herself.

After that his surprise returned. It was astonishing she should have given him up — astonishing to the point of annoyance. A great many women in Paris, some as well-born, most far prettier and more intelligent than the little Contesse, would have been proud of his preference. Flore, an artist to her finger-tips, good, gay, witty, with the warmest heart you could desire, the most cultivated mind, only longed to be allowed to serve him. And he had eluded them all, had treated Flore with studied coldness, for the sake of this little girl, who now dared to play him false — after letting him wait for her seven years, just when the moment had come to claim the fulfilment of her promise.

Beneath a calm exterior his thoughts travelled with stormy rapidity. What unexampled impudence on the part of the father, what treachery in the daughter! His anger augmented. He could no longer conceal it; for his armor of polished coldness was but a weapon of defence painfully acquired. The color rose all over his face, and his ireful eyes fixed themselves on August as though he saw in him the chief cause of offence.

"Go to Berlin," Harms urged; "you will yet be in time."

"Do you imagine I should beseech her to reconsider, to marry me after all? No. I think myself fortunate in discovering, before it is too late, the falseness and vacuity of which she is capable. But I will go to Berlin and see her. I owe this to myself. She shall not ease her conscience by saying I made no claim."

"Yes, I will see her," he reflected. "I will reproach her to her face." He foresaw in this interview a new experience which would be instructive to him. Still, as when a child, he sought curiously for emotions, and was eager to exalt, to intoxicate, to crucify his heart for the pleasure of standing aside to watch the effects. He purposely worked himself into the delusion that he still loved Marie von Dittenheim with passion, in order that the sensations of the final interview might be the more intense.

He began at once to prepare for departure. Harms desired to accompany him, and Emil permitted him to do so, not caring sufficiently for his absence to find it worth while to forbid his presence. He kissed his women-kind without affection, and turned his back on Klettendorf without regret. It happened that he never saw either village or kindred again.

He made the journey to Berlin in impenetrable silence, — arranging the phrases he should make use of in the coming scene, testing the bitter flavor of each word, selecting those that would inflict the sharpest pain.

Harms respected Schoenemann's silence. He knew so perfectly all that the renunciation of the beloved one means. His heart suffered vicariously for the suffering of his friend.

Berlin was reached late one evening, and the two men put up at a small hotel. Harms informed himself as to the quarter of the town the Dittenheims inhabited, its distance, and the way thither. He accompanied Emil next morning part of the way. "Take courage!" he said. "Be sure she still loves you;" and then, with a warm hand-grip, turned and left him.

It was March; an iron day. The streets were searched by a piercing wind, which tried even the stolid cheeriness of the Berliners. People walked with heads held low, wraps muffled up to nose and ears, hands encased in fur or woollen gloves, and still the universal enemy pierced into every chink and cranny, froze the marrow of their bones, and filled their eyes with dust. Not a propitious day for a wedding, if to-day it was, and yet the day poetic justice should select for the wedding of one who had broken plighted vows.

The Dittenheim house was large and handsome, with many windows looking on the street. Emil found the door standing half open, as though some one had hurriedly passed out or in. An immense basket of flowers stood in the hall. Other flowers, rows of tall white lilies, masses of white bridal roses, white narcissi, and white snowdrops, were heaped in disordered beauty against one wall. There was a sense of expectancy, a flavor of excitement in the air, as though some imposing ceremony were about to take place. Emil, going in, found none to question him. It seemed as though the household, thrown off its balance by the coming event, had abandoned its accustomed routine.

A door shut above. Looking up towards the gallery which ran round the upper floor, Schoenemann saw a young woman flit rapidly by. She was in a light-colored gown. She was not unlike Marie. He was convinced it was Marie. He hurried up the shallow steps. But before he reached the landing she had disappeared through one of the several doors which met his view.

An overpowering scent of flowers greeted him. Here and there on the crimson carpets lay a sprig of jasmine or a lily of the valley, as though such quantities had been carried up that the few which fell were left unheeded. The unfamiliar house in which he found himself, the silence, the fragrance, reminded Emil of that other day, so long ago, when he first visited Bellavista; then unknown to himself he was advancing to Love's birth. Now he told himself, with a bitterness he did not feel, he went to Love's grave.

Opposite to him, as he reached the head of the stairs, were high doors of white enamelled wood. They gave, presumably, on to the reception-rooms, the dozen windows of which overlooked the street. Here he should doubtless find Marie herself, or at least some one who could bring him to her. He opened one door-wing.

To his surprise he faced darkness, for the wind, rushing up from the hall, momentarily extinguished the six wax candles which stood in tall silver candlesticks down the centre of the floor. Emil took a step forward and closed the door behind him. The lights burned up again yellow and steady. They shed their radiance down on a mass of flowers, on a cloth of white satin . . . what was it? . . . an altar? . . . or a bed on which a woman was sleeping? . . . The next instant Emil saw it was a bier.

Advancing, he stood between the candles, looking down on the dead Marie. For he knew intuitively it was she, though at first his eyes denied it. She was so changed from the little moon-faced girl he remembered. She was beautified and ennobled by the hand of Death almost beyond recognition. Her features in their purer and finer outlines recalled those of her dead mother. Emil, who had looked at the Graefin and never seen her in the old days, saw her now, and admitted she was fairer than the little daughter who had stood beside her; but the dead girl who lay at his feet was even fairer than the mother. Nothing remained absolutely of the Marie he remembered but the light-brown crinkly hair, which, flowing down on either side of the pale face, was spread out over the coverlet to the slightly raised knees. The delicate waxen hands were crossed upon a crucifix, and on a satin ribbon round the neck hung a common crystal locket.

Emil had sought emotions: here he found

some of unexpected thrillingness. He was genuinely shaken. The charm of his lost love for Marie returned with full force. His heart seemed to melt, tears gushed from his eyes, all his cold self-sufficiency fell from him. Could the dead at that moment have come to life, he would have flung himself at her feet and sworn eternal devotion. The locket cherished to the end touched him inexpressibly. He recognized his own hair still within it. He knew she had worn it day and night upon her heart, and had wished it to go untouched with her to the grave. He remembered with compunction that the companion locket was long since lost. It had gone astray in one of his many Paris removals.

For the moment he hated himself. By the power which is given to the imaginative, he identified himself with the dead Marie. In the interval of a few seconds he lived through her entire life, loved with her, suffered with her. He understood how completely and irrevocably she had given up her personality to him, how to her gentle and faithful nature he had appeared the only man possible; he felt how constantly she had thought about him, how patiently she had waited and hoped, how the disappointment of his silence had only strengthened her love through pain. While he had been working, living, enjoying a thousand interests, or concentrating them all into the one absorbing pursuit, his image had been for her all in all. During these seven years, when he had forgotten her for months at a time, or only remembered her with coldness, every hour of every day her thoughts had turned to him. Love and hope had kept her alive, when otherwise she must long ago have fallen a victim to the hereditary disease which shed its fateful beauty upon her face. It was only when hope was crushed out, and she found herself on the point of ceding to the continuous pressure of relatives and circumstances, that she had given up the struggle and life both at once.

Down Emil's cheeks tears ran unchecked. Love, melancholy, and passionate regret flooded his soul. He gazed at the dead face, and to his shaken fantasy it seemed to regain warmth and color. He listened intently, and could have sworn he heard low and regular breathing. . . . But suddenly his heart stood still! A new force overwhelmed it. . . .

Meanwhile, a figure, sitting hitherto unnoticed in the darkness beyond the circle of candle-light, rose and came forward. It was Graf Dittenheim, but a changed, a broken man. His air of amused superiority, his ironical smile, were gone. Death for the moment had dragged him down to a level with his fellows. He and Emil exchanged glances of instant recognition. Surprise, doubt, a sort of remorse showed themselves on Dittenheim's countenance. He noticed the tears which still wetted the young man's face, and with a movement of the hand indicated the dead Marie.

"Is it possible you cared for her after all?" he said in a low voice; "that you have remained true?"

But Schoenemann only looked at him in silence and with an intense earnestness. Then he turned abruptly and walked out of the room. Out of the room, out of the house. Like one distraught he slipped through the streets of the city, and, meeting Harms on the tavern steps, flung him aside with furious impatience.

"Oh, for God's sake, leave me alone!" he cried violently; and Harms was not wounded. He saw that something terrible had happened, and he understood so well the hopeless misery that cries for solitude.

Meanwhile Emil double-locked the doors of

his room, fearful only that the unlucky encounter might have stemmed or diverted the torrent of music flowing within him. He seized pen and paper, and began to pour it forth in a series of spluttering dots and dashes. His brain was on fire with the excitement, his soul filled with the fierce joy which only the artist knows, and he in the moments of creation alone.

With the waning light the sketch lay complete, and Schoenemann threw himself back in his chair with a smile of supreme contentment. Then came the reaction; he yawned, felt inclined for supper, locked up his papers, and went down to seek Harms, who was stupefied by his friend's genial spirits. But the latter was happy, knowing that the work he had just completed was very good.

For it was thus that the famous "Elegie" came to be written. This is the story.

IRREMEDIABLE.

IRREMEDIABLE.

A YOUNG man strolled along a country road one August evening after a long delicious day — a day of that blessed idleness the man of leisure never knows: one must be a bank clerk forty-nine weeks out of the fifty-two before one can really appreciate the exquisite enjoyment of doing nothing for twelve hours at a stretch. Willoughby had spent the morning lounging about a sunny rickyard; then, when the heat grew unbearable, he had retreated to an orchard, where, lying on his back in the long cool grass, he had traced the pattern of the apple-leaves diapered above him upon the summer sky; now that the heat of the day was over, he had come to roam whither sweet fancy led him, to lean over gates, view the prospect, and meditate upon the pleasures of a well-spent day. Five such days had already passed over his head, fifteen more remained to him. Then farewell to freedom and clean country air! Back again to London and another year's toil.

He came to a gate on the right of the road. Behind it a footpath meandered up over a grassy slope. The sheep nibbling on its summit cast long shadows down the hill almost to his feet. Road and field-path were equally new to him, but the latter offered greener attractions; he vaulted lightly over the gate, and had so little idea he was taking thus the first step towards ruin that he began to whistle "White Wings" from pure joy of life.

The sheep stopped feeding, and raised their heads to stare at him from pale-lashed eyes; first one and then another broke into a startled run, until there was a sudden woolly stampede of the entire flock. When Willoughby gained the ridge from which they had just scattered, he came in sight of a woman sitting on a stile at the further end of the field. As he advanced towards her he saw that she was young, and that she was not what is called "a lady" — of which he was glad; an earlier episode in his career having indissolubly associated in his mind ideas of feminine refinement with those of feminine treachery.

He thought it probable this girl would be

willing to dispense with the formalities of an introduction, and that he might venture with her on some pleasant foolish chat.

As she made no movement to let him pass, he stood still, and, looking at her, began to smile.

She returned his gaze from unabashed dark eyes, and then laughed, showing teeth white, sound, and smooth as split hazel-nuts.

"Do you wanter get over?" she remarked, familiarly.

"I'm afraid I can't without disturbing you."

"Dontcher think you're much better where you are?" said the girl. On which Willoughby hazarded,—

"You mean to say looking at you? Well, perhaps I am!"

The girl at this laughed again, but nevertheless dropped herself down into the further field; then, leaning her arms upon the crossbar, she informed the young man, "No, I don't wanter spoil your walk. You were goin' p'raps ter Beacon Point? It's very pretty that wye."

"I was going nowhere in particular," he replied; "just exploring, so to speak. I'm a stranger in these parts."

"How funny! Imer stranger here too. I only come down larse Friday to stye with a Naunter mine in Horton. Are you stying in Horton?"

Willoughby told her he was not in Orton, but at Povey Cross Farm, out in the other direction.

"Oh, Mrs. Payne's, ain't it? I've heard aunt speak ovvre. She takes summer boarders, don't chee? I egspek you come from London, heh?"

"And I expect you come from London too?" said Willoughby, recognizing the familiar accent.

"You're as sharp as a needle," cried the girl, with her unrestrained laugh; "so I do. I'm here for a hollerday 'cos I was so done up with the work and the hot weather. I don't look as though I'd bin ill, do I? But I was, though; for it was just stiflin' hot up in our workrooms all larse month, an' tailorin's awful hard work at the bester times."

Willoughby felt a sudden accession of interest in her. Like many intelligent young men, he had dabbled a little in Socialism, and at one time had wandered among the dispossessed; but since then, had caught up and held loosely the new doctrine, — it is a good and fitting thing that Woman also should earn her bread by the sweat of her brow. Always in reference to the woman who, fifteen months before, had treated him ill, he had said to himself that even the breaking of stones in the road should be considered a more feminine employment than the breaking of hearts.

He gave way, therefore, to a movement of friendliness for this working daughter of the people, and joined her on the other side of the stile in token of his approval. She, twisting round to face him, leaned now with her back against the bar, and the sunset fires lent a fleeting glory to her face. Perhaps she guessed how becoming the light was, for she took off her hat and let it touch to gold the ends and fringes of her rough abundant hair. Thus and at this moment she made an agreeable picture, to which stood as background all the beautiful wooded Southshire view.

"You don't really mean to say you are a tailoress?" said Willoughby, with a sort of eager compassion.

"I do, though! An' I've bin one ever since I was fourteen. Look at my fingers if you don't b'lieve me."

She put out her right hand, and he took hold of it, as he was expected to do. The finger-ends were frayed and blackened by needle-pricks, but the hand itself was plump, moist, and not unshapely. She meanwhile examined Willoughby's fingers enclosing hers.

"It's easy ter see you've never done no work!" she said, half admiring, half envious. "I s'pose you're a tip-top swell, ain't you?"

"Oh, yes! I'm a tremendous swell indeed!" said Willoughby, ironically. He thought of his hundred and thirty pounds salary; and he mentioned his position in the British and Colonial Banking house, without shedding much illumination on her mind; for she insisted:

"Well, anyhow, you're a gentleman. I've often wished I was a lady. It must be so nice ter wear fine clo'es an' never have ter do any work all day long."

Willoughby thought it innocent of the girl to say this; it reminded him of his own notion as a child, — that kings and queens put on their crowns the first thing on rising in the morning. His cordiality rose another degree.

"If being a gentleman means having nothing to do," said he, smiling, "I can certainly lay no claim to the title. Life isn't all beer and skittles with me, any more than it is with you. Which is the better reason for enjoying the present moment, don't you think? Suppose, now, like a kind little girl, you were to show me the way to Beacon Point, which you say is so pretty?"

She required no further persuasion. As he walked beside her through the upland fields where the dusk was beginning to fall, and the white evening moths to emerge from their daytime hiding-places, she asked him many personal questions, most of which he thought fit to parry. Taking no offence thereat, she told him, instead, much concerning herself and her family. Thus he learned her name was Esther Stables, that she and her people lived Whitechapel way; that her father was seldom sober, and her mother always ill; and that the aunt with whom she was staying kept the post-office and general shop in Orton village. He learned, too, that Esther was discontented with life in general; that, though she hated being at home, she found the country dreadfully dull; and that, consequently, she was extremely glad to have made his acquaintance. But what he chiefly realized when they parted was that he had spent a couple of pleasant hours talking nonsense with a girl who was natural, simple-minded, and entirely free from that repellently protective atmosphere with which a woman of the "classes" so carefully surrounds herself. He and Esther had "made friends" with the ease and rapidity of children before they have learned the dread meaning of "etiquette," and they said good-night, not without some talk of meeting each other again.

Obliged to breakfast at a quarter to eight in town, Willoughby was always luxuriously late when in the country, where he took his meals also in leisurely fashion, often reading from a book propped up on the table before him. But the morning after his meeting with Esther Stables found him less disposed to read than usual. Her image obtruded itself upon the printed page, and at length grew so importunate he came to the conclusion the only way to lay it was to confront it with the girl herself.

Wanting some tobacco, he saw a good reason for going into Orton. Esther had told him he could get tobacco and everything else at her aunt's. He found the post-office to be one of the first houses in the widely spaced village street. In front of the cottage was a small garden ablaze with old-fashioned flowers; and in a larger garden at one side were apple-trees, raspberry and currant bushes, and six thatched beehives on a bench. The bowed windows of the little shop were partly screened by sun-blinds; nevertheless the lower panes still displayed a heterogeneous collection of goods,— lemons, hanks of yarn, white linen buttons upon blue cards, sugar cones, churchwarden pipes, and tobacco jars. A letter-box opened its narrow mouth low down in one wall, and over the door swung the sign, "Stamps and money-order office," in black letters on white enamelled iron.

The interior of the shop was cool and dark. A second glass-door at the back permitted Willoughby to see into a small sitting-room, and out again through a low and square-paned window to the sunny landscape beyond. Silhouetted against the light were the heads of two women: the rough young head of yesterday's Esther, the lean outline and bugled cap of Esther's aunt.

It was the latter who at the jingling of the door-bell rose from her work and came forward to serve the customer; but the girl, with much mute meaning in her eyes, and a finger laid upon her smiling mouth, followed behind.

Her aunt heard her footfall. "What do you want here, Esther?" she said, with thin disapproval; "get back to your sewing."

Esther gave the young man a signal seen only by him, and slipped out into the sidegarden, where he found her when his purchases were made. She leaned over the privet-hedge to intercept him as he passed.

"Aunt's an awful ole maid," she remarked apologetically; "I b'lieve sh' 'd never let me say a word to enny one if she could help it."

"So you got home all right last night?" Willoughby inquired; "what did your aunt say to you?"

"Oh, she arst me where I 'd been, and I tolder a lotter lies!" Then, with a woman's intuition, perceiving that this speech jarred, Esther made haste to add, "She's so dreadful hard on me! I dursn't tell her I 'd been with a gentleman, or she'd never have let me out alone again."

"And at present I suppose you 'll be found somewhere about that same stile every evening?" said Willoughby, foolishly, for he really did not much care whether he met her again or not. Now he was actually in her company, he was surprised at himself for having given her a whole morning's thought; yet the eagerness of her answer flattered him, too.

"To-night I can't come, worse luck! It's Thursday, and the shops here close of a Thursday at five. I'll havter keep aunt company. But to-morrer — I can be there to-morrer. You'll come, say?"

"Esther!" cried a vexed voice, and the precise, right-minded aunt emerged through a row of raspberry-bushes; "whatever are you thinking about, delayin' the gentleman in this fashion?" She was full of rustic and official civility for "the gentleman," but indignant with her niece. "I don't want none of your London manners down here," Willoughby heard her say as she marched the girl off.

He himself was not sorry to be released from Esther's too friendly eyes, and he spent an agreeable evening over a book, and this time managed to forget her completely.

Though he remembered her first thing next morning, it was to smile wisely and determine he would not meet her again. Yet by dinner-time the day seemed long; why, after all, should he not meet her? By tea-time prudence triumphed anew — no, he would not go. Then he drank his tea hastily and set off for the stile.

Esther was waiting for him. Expectation had given an additional color to her cheeks, and her red-brown hair showed here and there a beautiful glint of gold. He could not help admiring the vigorous way in which it waved and twisted, or the little curls which grew at the nape of her neck, tight and close as those of a young lamb's fleece. Her neck here was admirable, too, in its smooth creaminess; and when her eyes lighted up with such evident pleasure at his coming, how avoid the conviction she was a good and nice girl after all?

He proposed they should go down into the little copse on the right, where they would be less disturbed by the occasional passer-by. Here, seated on a felled tree-trunk, Willoughby began that bantering, silly, meaningless form of conversation known among the "classes" as flirting. He had but the wish to make himself agreeable, and to while away the time. Esther, however, misunderstood him.

Willoughby's hand lay palm downwards on his knee, and she, noticing a ring which he wore on his little finger, took hold of it.

"What a funny ring!" she said; "let's look?"

To disembarrass himself of her touch, he pulled the ring off and gave it her to examine.

"What's that ugly dark green stone?" she asked.

"It's called a sardonyx."

"What's it for?" she said, turning it about.

"It's a signet ring, to seal letters with."

"An' there's a sorter king's head scratched on it, an' some writin' too, only I carnt make it out?"

"It isn't the head of a king, although it wears a crown," Willoughby explained, "but the head and bust of a Saracen against whom my ancestor of many hundred years ago went to fight in the Holy Land. And the words cut round it are our motto, 'Vertue vuanceth,' which means, Virtue prevails."

Willoughby may have displayed some accession of dignity in giving this bit of family history, for Esther fell into uncontrolled laughter, at which he was much displeased. And when the girl made as though she would put the ring on her own finger, asking, "Shall I keep it?" he colored up with sudden annoyance.

"It was only my fun!" said Esther, hastily, and gave him the ring back; but his cordiality was gone. He felt no inclination to renew the idle-word pastime, said it was time to go, and, swinging his cane vexedly, struck off the heads of the flowers and the weeds as he went. Esther walked by his side in complete silence, a phenomenon of which he presently became conscious. He felt rather ashamed of having shown temper.

"Well, here's your way home," said he, with an effort at friendliness. "Good-by; we've had a nice evening, anyhow. It was pleasant down there in the woods, eh?"

He was astonished to see her eyes soften with tears, and to hear the real emotion in her voice as she answered, "It was just heaven down there with you until you turned so funny-like. What had I done to make you cross? Say you forgive me, do!"

"Silly child!" said Willoughby, completely mollified, "I'm not the least angry. There, good-by!" and, like a fool, he kissed her.

He anathematized his folly in the white light of next morning, and, remembering the kiss he had given her, repented it very sincerely. He had an uncomfortable suspicion she had not received it in the same spirit in which it had been bestowed, but, attaching more serious meaning to it, would build expectations thereon which must be left unfulfilled. It was best indeed not to meet her again; for he acknowledged to himself that, though he only half liked, and even slightly feared her, there was a certain attraction about her — was it in her dark unflinching eyes, or in her very red lips? — which might lead him into greater follies still.

Thus it came about that for two successive evenings Esther waited for him in vain; and on the third evening he said to himself with a grudging relief that by this time she had probably transferred her affections to some one else.

It was Saturday, the second Saturday since he left town. He spent the day about the farm, contemplated the pigs, inspected the feeding of the stock, and assisted at the afternoon milking. Then at evening, with a refilled pipe, he went for a long lean over the west gate, while he traced fantastic pictures and wove romances in the glories of the sunset clouds.

He watched the colors glow from gold to scarlet, change to crimson, sink at last to sad purple reefs and isles, when the sudden consciousness of some one being near him made him turn round. There stood Esther, and her eyes were full of eagerness and anger.

"Why have you never been to the stile again?" she asked him. "You promised to come faithful, and you never came. Why have you not kep' your promise? Why?—why?" she persisted, stamping her foot because Willoughby remained silent.

What could he say? Tell her she had no business to follow him like this; or own, what was, unfortunately, the truth, he was just a little glad to see her?

"P'raps you don't care for me any more?" she said. "Well, why did you kiss me, then?"

Why, indeed! thought Willoughby, marvelling at his own idiotcy, and yet — such is the inconsistency of man — not wholly without the desire to kiss her again. And while he looked at her she suddenly flung herself down on the hedge-bank at his feet and burst into tears. She did not cover up her face, but simply pressed one cheek down upon the grass while the water poured from her eyes with astonishing abundance. Willoughby saw the dry earth turn dark and moist as it drank the tears in. This, his first experience of Esther's powers of weeping, distressed him horribly; never in his life before had he seen any one weep like that; he should not have believed such a thing possible. He was alarmed, too, lest she should be noticed from the house. He opened the gate. "Esther!" he begged, "don't cry. Come out here, like a dear girl, and let us talk sensibly."

Because she stumbled, unable to see her way through wet eyes, he gave her his hand, and they found themselves in a field of corn, walking along the narrow grass-path that skirted it, in the shadow of the hedgerow.

"What is there to cry about because you have not seen me for two days?" he began. "Why, Esther, we are only strangers, after all. When we have been at home a week or two we shall scarcely remember each other's names."

Esther sobbed at intervals, but her tears had ceased. "It's fine for you to talk of home," she said to this. "You've got something that is a home, I s'pose? But me! my home's like hell, with nothing but quarrellin' and cursin', and father who beats us whether sober or drunk. Yes!" she repeated shrewdly, seeing the lively disgust on Willoughby's face, "he beat me, all ill as I was, jus' before I come away. I could show you the bruises on my arms still. And now to go back there after knowin' you! It'll be worse than ever. I can't endure it, and I won't! I'll put an end to it or myself somehow, I swear!"

"But, my poor Esther, how can I help it, what can I do?" said Willoughby. He was greatly moved, full of wrath with her father, with all the world which makes women suffer. He had suffered himself at the hands of a woman, and severely; but this, instead of hardening his heart, had only rendered it the more supple. And yet he had a vivid perception of the peril in which he stood. An interior voice urged him to break away, to seek safety in flight even at the cost of appearing cruel or ridiculous; so, coming to a point in the field where an elm-bole jutted out across the path, he saw with relief he could now withdraw his hand from the girl's, since they must walk singly to skirt round it.

Esther took a step in advance, stopped, and suddenly turned to face him; she held out her two hands, and her face was very near his own.

"Don't you care for me one little bit?" she said wistfully; and surely sudden madness fell upon him. For he kissed her again, he kissed her many times, he took her in his arms, and pushed all thoughts of the consequences far from him.

But when, an hour later, he and Esther stood by the last gate on the road to Orton, some of these consequences were already calling loudly to him.

"You know I have only £130 a year?" he told her; "it's no very brilliant prospect for you to marry me on that."

For he had actually offered her marriage, although to the mediocre man such a proceeding must appear incredible, uncalled for. But to Willoughby, overwhelmed with sadness and remorse, it seemed the only atonement possible.

Sudden exultation leaped at Esther's heart.

"O! I'm used to managin'," she told him confidently, and mentally resolved to buy herself, so soon as she was married, a black feather boa, such as she had coveted last winter.

Willoughby spent the remaining days of his holiday in thinking out and planning with Esther the details of his return to London and her own, the secrecy to be observed, the necessary legal steps to be taken, and the quiet suburb in which they would set up housekeeping. And, so successfully did he carry out his arrangements, that within five weeks from the day on which he had first met Esther Stables he and she came out one morning from a church in Highbury, husband and wife. It was a mellow September day, the streets were filled with sunshine, and Willoughby, in reckless high spirits, imagined he saw a reflection of his own gayety on the indifferent faces of the passers-by. There being no one else to perform the office, he congratulated himself very warmly, and Esther's frequent laughter filled in the pauses of the day.

Three months later Willoughby was dining with a friend, and the hour-hand of the clock nearing ten, the host no longer resisted the guest's growing anxiety to be gone. He arose and exchanged with him good wishes and good-by.

"Marriage is evidently a most successful institution," said he, half jesting, half sincere; "you almost make me inclined to go and get married myself. Confess now your thoughts have been at home the whole evening?"

Willoughby thus addressed turned red to the roots of his hair, but did not deny it.

IRREMEDIABLE.

The other laughed. "And very commendable they should be," he continued, "since you are scarcely, so to speak, out of your honeymoon."

With a social smile on his lips, Willoughby calculated a moment before replying, "I have been married exactly three months and three days." Then, after a few words respecting their next meeting, the two shook hands and parted, the young host to finish the evening with books and pipe, the young husband to set out on a twenty minutes' walk to his home.

It was a cold clear December night following a day of rain. A touch of frost in the air had dried the pavements, and Willoughby's footfall ringing upon the stones re-echoed down the empty suburban street. Above his head was a dark remote sky thickly powdered with stars, and as he turned westward Alpherat hung for a moment "comme le point sur un *i*," over the slender spire of St. John's. But he was insensible to the worlds about him; he was absorbed in his own thoughts, and these, as his friend had surmised, were entirely with his wife. For Esther's face was always before his eyes, her voice was always in his ears, she filled the universe for him; yet only four months ago he had never seen her, had never heard her name. This was the curious part of it — here in December he found himself the husband of a girl who was completely dependent upon him not only for food, clothes, and lodging, but for her present happiness, her whole future life; and last July he had been scarcely more than a boy himself, with no greater care on his mind than the pleasant difficulty of deciding where he should spend his annual three weeks' holiday.

But it is events, not months or years, which age. Willoughby, who was only twenty-six, remembered his youth as a sometime companion irrevocably lost to him; its vague delightful hopes were now crystallized into definite ties, and its happy irresponsibilities displaced by a sense of care inseparable perhaps from the most fortunate of marriages.

As he reached the street in which he lodged his pace involuntarily slackened. While still some distance off, his eye sought out and distinguished the windows of the room in which Esther awaited him. Through the broken slats of the Venetian blinds he could see the yellow gaslight within. The parlor beneath was in darkness; his landlady had evidently gone to bed, there being no light over the hall-door either. In some apprehension he consulted his watch under the last street-lamp he passed, to find comfort in assuring himself it was only ten minutes after ten. He let himself in with his latch-key, hung up his hat and overcoat by the sense of touch, and, groping his way upstairs, opened the door of the first-floor sitting-room.

At the table in the centre of the room sat his wife, leaning upon her elbows, her two hands thrust up into her ruffled hair; spread out before her was a crumpled yesterday's newspaper, and so interested was she to all appearance in its contents that she neither spoke nor looked up as Willoughby entered. Around her were the still uncleared tokens of her last meal: tea-slops, bread-crumbs, and an eggshell crushed to fragments upon a plate, which was one of those trifles that set Willoughby's teeth on edge — whenever his wife ate an egg she persisted in turning the egg-cup upside down upon the tablecloth, and pounding the shell to pieces in her plate with her spoon.

The room was repulsive in its disorder. The one lighted burner of the gaselier, turned too high, hissed up into a long tongue of flame. The fire smoked feebly under a newly administered shovelful of "slack," and a heap of ashes and cinders littered the grate. A pair of walking boots, caked in dry mud, lay on the hearth-rug just where they had been thrown off. On the mantelpiece, amidst a dozen other articles which had no business there, was a bedroom-candlestick; and every single article of furniture stood crookedly out of its place.

Willoughby took in the whole intolerable picture, and yet spoke with kindliness. "Well, Esther! I'm not so late, after all. I hope you did not find the time dull by yourself?" Then he explained the reason of his absence. He had met a friend he had not seen for a couple of years, who had insisted on taking him home to dine.

His wife gave no sign of having heard him; she kept her eyes riveted on the paper before her.

"You received my wire, of course," Willoughby went on, "and did not wait?"

Now she crushed the newspaper up with a passionate movement, and threw it from her. She raised her head, showing cheeks blazing with anger, and dark, sullen, unflinching eyes.

"I did wyte then!" she cried. "I wyted till near eight before I got your old telegraph! I s'pose that's what you call the manners of a 'gentleman,' to keep your wife mewed up here, while you go gallivantin' off with your fine friends?"

Whenever Esther was angry, which was often, she taunted Willoughby with being "a gentleman," although this was the precise point about him which at other times found most favor in her eyes. .But to-night she was envenomed by the idea he had been enjoying himself without her, stung by fear lest he should have been in company with some other woman.

Willoughby, hearing the taunt, resigned himself to the inevitable. Nothing that he could do might now avert the breaking storm, all his words would only be twisted into fresh griefs. But sad experience had taught him that to take refuge in silence was more fatal still. When Esther was in such a mood as this it was best to supply the fire with fuel, that, through the very violence of the conflagration, it might the sooner burn itself out.

So he said what soothing things he could, and Esther caught them up, disfigured them, and flung them back at him with scorn. She reproached him with no longer caring for her; she vituperated the conduct of his family in never taking the smallest notice of her marriage; and she detailed the insolence of the landlady, who had told her that morning she pitied "poor Mr. Willoughby," and had refused to go out and buy herrings for Esther's early dinner.

Every affront or grievance, real or imaginary, since the day she and Willoughby had first met, she poured forth with a fluency due to frequent repetition, for, with the exception of to-day's added injuries, Willoughby had heard the whole litany many times before.

While she raged and he looked at her, he remembered he had once thought her pretty. He had seen beauty in her rough brown hair, her strong coloring, her full red mouth. He fell into musing . . . a woman may lack beauty, he told himself, and yet be loved. . . .

Meanwhile Esther reached white heats of passion, and the strain could no longer be sustained. She broke into sobs, and began to shed tears with the facility peculiar to her. In a moment her face was all wet with the big drops which rolled down her cheeks faster and faster, and fell with audible splashes on to the table, on to her lap, on to the floor. To this tearful abundance, formerly a surprising spectacle, Willoughby was now acclimatized; but the remnant of chivalrous feeling not yet extinguished in his bosom forbade him to sit stolidly by while a woman wept, without seeking to console her. As on previous occasions, his peace-overtures were eventually accepted. Esther's tears gradually ceased to flow, she began to exhibit a sort of compunction, she wished to be forgiven, and, with the kiss of reconciliation, passed into a phase of demonstrative affection perhaps more trying to Willoughby's patience than all that had preceded it. "You don't love me?" she questioned, "I'm sure you don't love me?" she reiterated; and he asseverated that he loved her until he despised himself. Then at last, only half satisfied, but wearied out with vexation — possibly, too, with a movement of pity at the sight of his haggard face — she consented to leave him. Only what was he going to do? she asked suspiciously; write those rubbishing stories of his? Well, he must promise not to stay up more than half an hour at the latest — only until he had smoked one pipe!

Willoughby promised, as he would have promised anything on earth to secure to himself a half-hour's peace and solitude. Esther groped for her slippers, which were kicked off under the table; scratched four or five matches along the box and threw them away before she succeeded in lighting her candle; set it down again to contemplate her tear-swollen reflection in the chimney-glass, and burst out laughing.

"What a fright I do look, to be sure!" she remarked complacently, and again thrust her two hands up through her disordered curls. Then, holding the candle at such an angle that the grease ran over on to the carpet, she gave Willoughby another vehement kiss, and trailed out of the room with an ineffectual attempt to close the door behind her.

Willoughby got up to shut it himself, and wondered why it was that Esther never did any one mortal thing efficiently or well. Good God! how irritable he felt! It was impossible to write. He must find an outlet for his impatience, rend or mend something. He began to straighten the room, but a wave of disgust came over him before the task was fairly commenced. What was the use? To-morrow all would be bad as before. What was the use of doing anything! He sat down by the table and leaned his head upon his hands.

The past came back to him in pictures; his boyhood's past first of all. He saw again the old home, every inch of which was familiar to him as his own name; he reconstructed in his thought all the old well-known furniture, and replaced it precisely as it had stood long ago. He passed again a childish finger over the rough surface of the faded Utrecht velvet chairs, and smelled again the strong fragrance of the white lilac-tree, blowing in through the open parlor-window. He savored anew the pleasant mental atmosphere produced by the dainty neatness of cultured women, the companionship of a few good pictures, of a few good books. Yet this home had been broken up years ago, the dear familiar things had been scattered far and wide, never to find themselves under the same roof again; and from those near relatives who still remained to him he lived now hopelessly estranged.

Then came the past of his first love-dream, when he worshipped at the feet of Nora Beresford, and, with the whole-heartedness of the true fanatic, clothed his idol with every imaginable attribute of virtue and tenderness. To this day there remained a secret shrine in his heart wherein the lady of his young ideal was still enthroned, although it was long since he had come to perceive she had nothing whatever in common with the Nora of reality. For the real Nora he had no longer any sentiment, she had passed altogether out of his life and thoughts; and yet, so permanent is all influence, whether good or evil, that the effect she wrought upon his character remained. He recognized to-night that her treatment of him in the past did not count for nothing among the various factors which had determined his fate.

Now, the past of only last year returned, and, strangely enough, this seemed farther removed from him than all the rest. He had been particularly strong, well, and happy this time last year. Nora was dismissed from his mind, and he had thrown all his energies into his work. His tastes were sane and simple, and his dingy furnished rooms had become through habit very pleasant to him. In being his own they were invested with a greater charm than another man's castle. Here he had smoked and studied, here he had made many a glorious voyage into the land of books. Many a home-coming, too, rose up before him out of the dark ungenial streets to a clean blazing fire, a neatly laid cloth, an evening of ideal enjoyment; many a summer twilight when he mused at the open window, plunging his gaze deep into the recesses of his neighbor's lime-tree, where the unseen sparrows chattered with such unflagging gayety.

He had always been given to much daydreaming, and it was in the silence of his rooms of an evening that he turned his phantasmal adventures into stories for the magazines; here had come to him many an editorial refusal, but here, too, he had received the news of his first unexpected success. All his happiest memories were embalmed in those shabby, badly furnished rooms.

Now all was changed. Now might there be no longer any soft indulgence of the hour's mood. His rooms and everything he owned belonged now to Esther too. She had objected to most of his photographs, and had removed them. She hated books, and were he ever so ill-advised as to open one in her presence, she immediately began to talk, no matter how silent or how sullen her previous mood had been. If he read aloud to her she either yawned despairingly, or was tickled into laughter where there was no reasonable cause. At first, Willoughby had tried to educate her, and had gone hopefully to the task. It is so natural to think you may make what you will of the woman who loves you. But Esther had no wish to improve. She evinced all the self-satisfaction of an illiterate mind. To her husband's gentle admonitions she replied with brevity that she thought her way quite as good as his; or, if he did n't approve of her pronunciation, he might do the other thing, she was too old to go to school again. He gave up the attempt, and, with humiliation at his previous fatuity, perceived that it was folly to expect that a few weeks of his companionship could alter or pull up the impressions of years, or rather of generations.

Yet here he paused to admit a curious thing: it was not only Esther's bad habits which vexed him, but habits quite unblameworthy in themselves, which he never would have noticed in another, irritated him in her. He disliked her manner of standing, of walking, of sitting in a chair, of folding her hands. Like a lover, he was conscious of her proximity without seeing her. Like a lover, too, his eyes followed her every movement, his ear noted every change in her voice. But, then, instead of being charmed by everything as the lover is, everything jarred upon him.

What was the meaning of this? To-night the anomaly pressed upon him; he reviewed his position. Here was he, quite a young man, just twenty-six years of age, married to Esther, and bound to live with her so long as life should last — twenty, forty, perhaps fifty years more. Every day of those years to be spent in her society; he and she face to face, soul to soul; they two alone amid all the whirling, busy, indifferent world. So near together in semblance, in truth so far apart as regards all that makes life dear.

Willoughby groaned. From the woman he did not love, whom he had never loved, he might not again go free; so much he recognized. The feeling he had once entertained for Esther, strange compound of mistaken chivalry and flattered vanity, was long since extinct; but what, then, was the sentiment with which she inspired him? For he was not indifferent to her — no, never for one instant could he persuade himself he was indifferent, never for one instant could he banish her from his thoughts. His mind's eye followed her during his hours of absence as pertinaciously as his bodily eye dwelt upon her actual presence. She was the principal object of the universe to him, the centre around which his wheel of life revolved with an appalling fidelity.

What did it mean? What could it mean? he asked himself with anguish.

And the sweat broke out upon his forehead and his hands grew cold, for on a sudden the truth lay there like a written word upon the tablecloth before him. This woman, whom he had taken to himself for better, for worse, inspired him with a passion — intense indeed, all-masterful, soul-subduing as Love itself. . . . But when he understood the terror of his Hatred, he laid his head upon his arms and wept, not facile tears like Esther's, but tears wrung out from his agonizing, unavailing regret.

POOR COUSIN LOUIS.

POOR COUSIN LOUIS.

THERE stands in the Islands a house known as "Les Calais." It has stood there already some three hundred years, and to judge from its stout walls and weather-tight appearance, promises to stand some three hundred more. Built of brown home-quarried stone, with solid stone chimney-stacks and roof of red tiles, its door is set in the centre beneath a semicircular arch of dressed granite, on the keystone of which is deeply cut the date of construction:

J V N I
1 6 0 3

Above the date straggle the letters, L G M M, initials of the forgotten names of the builder of the house and of the woman he married. In the summer weather of 1603 that inscription was cut, and the man and woman doubtless read it with pride and pleasure as they stood looking up at their fine new homestead. They believed it would carry their names down to posterity when they themselves should be gone; yet there stand the initials to-day, while the personalities they represent are as lost to memory as are the builders' graves.

At the moment when this little sketch opens, Les Calais had belonged for three generations to the family of Renouf (pronounced Rennuf), and it is with the closing days of Mr. Louis Renouf that it purposes to deal. But first to complete the description of the house, which is typical of the Islands: hundreds of such homesteads, placed singly or in groups — then sharing in one common name — may be found there in a day's walk, although it must be added that a day's walk almost suffices to explore any one of the Islands from end to end.

Les Calais shares its name with none. It stands alone, completely hidden, save at one point only, by its ancient elms. On either side of the doorway are two windows, each of twelve small panes, and there is a row of five similar windows above. Around the back and sides of the house cluster all sorts of outbuildings, necessary dependencies of a time when men made their own cider and candles, baked their own bread, cut and stacked their own wood, and dried the dung of their herds for extra winter fuel. Beyond the outbuildings lie its vegetable and fruit gardens, which again are surrounded on every side by its many rich vergées of pasture land.

Would you find Les Calais, take the highroad from Jacques-le-Port to the village of St. Gilles, then keep to the left of the schools along a narrow lane cut between high hedges. It is a cart-track only, as the deep sun-baked ruts testify, leading direct from St. Gilles to Vauvert, and, likely enough, during the whole of that distance you will not meet with a solitary person. You will see nothing but the green running hedgerows on either hand, the blue-domed sky above, from whence the lark, a black pin-point in the blue, flings down a gush of song; while the thrush you have disturbed lunching off that succulent snail takes short ground flights before you, at every pause turning back an ireful eye to judge how much farther you intend to pursue him. He is happy if you branch off midway to the left, down the lane leading straight to Les Calais.

A gable end of the house faces this lane, and its one window in the days of Louis Renouf looked out upon a dilapidated farm and stable-yard, the gate of which, turned back upon its hinges, stood wide open to the world. Within might be seen granaries empty of grain, stables where no horses fed, a long cow-house crumbling into ruin, and the broken stone sections of a cider-trough dismantled more than half a century back. Cushions of emerald moss studded the thatches, and Lilliputian forests of grass-blades sprang thick between the cobble-stones. The place might have been mistaken for some deserted grange but for the contradiction conveyed in a bright pewter full-bellied water-can standing near the well, in a pile of firewood, with chopper still stuck in the topmost billet, and in a tatterdemalion troop of barn-door fowl lagging meditatively across the yard.

On a certain day, when summer warmth and unbroken silence brooded over all, and the broad sunshine blent the yellows, reds, and grays of tile and stone, the greens of grass and foliage into one harmonious whole, a visitor entered the open gate. This was a tall, large young woman, with a fair, smooth, thirty-year-old face. Dressed in what was obviously her Sunday best, although it was neither Sunday nor even market-day, she wore a bonnet diademed with gas-green lilies of the valley, a netted black mantilla, and a velvet-trimmed violet silk gown, which she carefully lifted out of dust's way, thus displaying a stiffly starched petticoat and kid spring-side boots.

Such attire, unbeautiful in itself and incongruous with its surroundings, jarred harshly upon the picturesque note of the scene. From being a subject to perpetuate on canvas, it shrunk, as it were, to the background of a cheap photograph, or the stage adjuncts to the heroine of a farce. The silence too was shattered as the new-comer's foot fell upon the stones. An unseen dog began to mouth a joyous welcome, and the fowls, lifting their thin, apprehensive faces towards her, flopped into a clumsy run as though their last hour were visible.

The visitor meanwhile turned familiar steps to a door in the wall on the left, and, raising the latch, entered the flower-garden of Les Calais. This garden, lying to the south, consisted then, and perhaps does still, of two square grass-plots with a broad gravel path running round them and up to the centre of the house.

In marked contrast with the neglect of the farm-yard was this exquisitely kept garden, brilliant and fragrant with flowers. From a raised bed in the centre of each plot standard rose-trees shed out gorgeous perfume from chalices of every shade of loveliness, and thousands of white pinks justled shoulder to shoulder in narrow bands cut within the borders of the grass.

Busy over these, his back towards her, was an elderly man, braces hanging, in colored cotton shirt.

"Good afternoon, Tourtel," cried the lady, advancing.

Thus addressed, he straightened himself slowly and turned round. Leaning on his hoe, he shaded his eyes with his hand. "Eh den! it's you, Missis Pedvinn," said he; "but we did n't expec' you till to-morrow?"

"No, it's true," said Mrs. Poidevin, "that I wrote I would come Saturday, but Pedvinn expects some friends by the English boat, and wants me to receive them. Yet as they may be staying the week, I did not like to put poor Cousin Louis off so long without a visit, so thought I had better come up to-day."

Almost unconsciously, her phrases assumed apologetic form. She had an uneasy feeling Tourtel's wife might resent her unexpected advent; although why Mrs. Tourtel should object, or why she herself should stand in any awe of the Tourtels, she could not have explained. Tourtel was but gardener, the wife housekeeper and nurse, to her cousin Louis Renouf, master of Les Calais. "I sha'n't inconvenience Mrs. Tourtel, I hope? Of course I should n't think of staying tea if she is busy; I'll just sit an hour with Cousin Louis, and catch the six o'clock omnibus home from Vauvert."

Tourtel stood looking at her with wooden countenance, in which two small shifting eyes alone gave signs of life. "Eh, but you won't be no inconvenience to de ole woman, ma'am," said he, suddenly, in so loud a voice that Mrs. Poidevin jumped; "only de apple-gôche, dat she was goin' to bake agen your visit, won't be ready, dat's all."

He turned, and stared up at the front of the house; Mrs. Poidevin, for no reason at all, did so too. Door and windows were open wide. In the upper story, the white roller-blinds were let down against the sun, and on the broad sills of the parlor windows were nosegays placed in blue china jars. A white trelliswork criss-crossed over the façade, for the support of climbing rose and purple clematis which hung out a curtain of blossom almost concealing the masonry behind. The whole place breathed of peace and beauty, and Louisa Poidevin was lapped round with that pleasant sense of well-being which it was her chief desire in life never to lose. Though poor Cousin Louis — feeble, childish, solitary — was so much to be pitied, at least in his comfortable home and his worthy Tourtels he found compensation.

An instant after Tourtel had spoken, a woman passed across the wide hall. She had on a blue linen skirt, white stockings, and shoes of gray list. The strings of a large, bibbed, lilac apron drew the folds of a flowered bed-jacket about her ample waist; and her thick yellow-gray hair, worn without a cap, was arranged smoothly on either side of a narrow head. She just glanced out, and Mrs. Poidevin was on the point of calling to her, when Tourtel fell into a torrent of words about his flowers. He had so much to say on the subject of horticulture; was so anxious for her to examine the freesia bulbs lying in the tool-house, just separated from the spring plants; he denounced so fiercely the grinding policy of Brehault, the middleman, who purchased his garden stuff to resell it at Covent Garden — "my good! on dem freesias I did n't make not two doubles a bunch!" — that for a long quarter of an hour all memory of her cousin was driven from Mrs. Poidevin's brain. Then a voice said at her elbow, "Mr. Rennuf is quite ready to see you, ma'am," and there stood Tourtel's wife, with pale composed face, square shoulders and hips, and feet that moved noiselessly in her list slippers.

"Ah, Mrs. Tourtel, how do you do?" said the visitor; a question which in the Islands is no mere formula, but demands and obtains a detailed answer, after which the questioner's own health is politely inquired into. Not until this ceremony had been scrupulously accomplished, and the two women were on their way to the house, did Mrs. Poidevin beg to know how things were going with her "poor cousin."

There lay something at variance between the ruthless, calculating spirit which looked forth from the housekeeper's cold eye, and the extreme suavity of her manner of speech.

"Eh, my good! but much de same, ma'am, in his health, an' more fancies dan ever in his head. First one ting an' den anudder, an' always tinking dat everybody is robbin' him. You rem-ember de larse time you was here, an' Mister Rennuf was abed? Well, den, after you was gone, if he didn't deck-clare you had taken some of de fedders of his bed away wid you. Yes, my good! he tought you had cut a hole in de tick as you sat dere beside him an' emptied de fedders away into your pocket."

Mrs. Poidevin was much interested. "Dear me, is it possible? . . . But it's quite a mania with him. I remember now, on that very day he complained to me Tourtel was wearing his shirts, and wanted me to go in with him to Lepage's to order some new ones."

"Eh! but what would Tourtel want wid fine white shirts like dem?" said the wife, placidly. "But Mr. Louis have such dozens an' dozens of 'em dat dey gets hidden away in de presses, an' he tinks dem stolen."

They reached the house. The interior is as characteristic of the Islands as is the outside. Two steps take you down into the hall, crossing the further end of which is the staircase with its balustrade of carved black oak. Instead of the mean painted sticks, known technically as "raisers," and connected together at the top by a vulgar mahogany handrail — a fundamental article of faith with the modern builder — these old Island balustrades are formed of wooden panels, fretted out into scrolls, representing flower or leaf or curious beaked and winged creatures, which go curving, creeping, and ramping along in the direction of the stairs. In every house you will find the detail different, while each resembles all as a whole. For in the old days the workman, were he never so humble, recognized the possession of an individual mind, as well as of two eyes and two hands, and he translated fearlessly this individuality of his into his work. Every house built in those days and existing down to these, is not only a confession, in some sort, of the tastes, the habits, the character, of the man who planned it, but preserves a record likewise of every one of the subordinate minds employed in the various parts.

Off the hall of Les Calais are two rooms on the left and one on the right. The solidity of early seventeenth-century walls is shown in the embrasure depth (measuring fully three feet) of windows and doors. Up to fifty years ago all the windows had leaded casements, as had every similar Island dwelling-house. To-day, to the artist's regret, he will hardly find one. The showy taste of the Second Empire spread from Paris even to these remote parts, and plate-glass, or at least oblong panes, everywhere replaced the mediæval style. In 1854, Louis Renouf, just three and thirty, was about to bring his bride, Miss Betsy Mauger, home to the old house. In her honor it was done up throughout, and the diamonded casements were replaced by guillotine windows, six panes to each sash.

The best parlor then became a "drawing-room;" its raftered ceiling was whitewashed, and its great centre-beam of oak infamously papered to match the walls. The newly married couple were not in a position to refurnish in approved Second Empire fashion. The gilt and marble, the console tables and mirrors, the impossibly curved sofas and chairs, were for the moment beyond them; the wife promised herself to acquire these later on. But later on came a brood of sickly children (only one of whom reached manhood); to the consequent expenses Les Calais owed the preservation of its inlaid wardrobes, its four-post bedsteads with slender fluted columns, and its Chippendale parlor chairs, the backs of which simulate a delicious intricacy of twisted ribbons. As a little girl, Louisa Poidevin had often amused herself studying these convolutions, and seeking to puzzle out among the rippling ribbons some beginning or some end; but as she grew up, even the simplest problem lost interest for her, and the sight of the old Chippendale chairs standing along the walls of the large parlor scarcely stirred her bovine mind now to so much as reminiscence.

It was the door of this large parlor that the housekeeper opened as she announced, "Here is Mrs. Pedvinn come to see you, sir," and followed the visitor in.

Sitting in a capacious "berceuse," stuffed and chintz-covered, was the shrunken figure of a more than seventy-year-old man. He was wrapped in a worn gray dressing-gown, with a black velvet skull-cap napless at the seams, covering his spiritless hair, and he looked out upon his narrow world from dim eyes set in cavernous orbits. In their expression was something of the questioning timidity of a child, contrasting curiously with the querulousness of old age shown in the thin sucked-in lips, now and again twitched by a movement in unison with the twitching of the withered hands spread out upon his knees.

The sunshine, slanting through the low windows, bathed hands and knees, lean shanks and slippered feet, in mote-flecked streams of gold. It bathed anew rafters and ceiling-beam, as it had bathed them at the same hour and season these last three hundred years; it played over the worm-eaten furniture, and lent transitory color to the faded samplers on the walls, bringing into prominence one particular sampler, which depicted in silks Adam and Eve seated beneath the fatal tree, and recorded the fact that Marie Hochedé was seventeen in 1808 and put her "trust in God;" and the same ray kissed the cheek of that very Marie's son who at the time her girlish fingers pricked the canvas belonged to the enviable myriads of the unthought-of and the unborn.

"Why, how cold you are, Cousin Louis," said Mrs. Poidevin, taking his passive hand between her two warm ones, and feeling a chill strike from it through the violet kid gloves; "and in spite of all this sunshine too!"

"Ah, I'm not always in the sunshine," said the old man; "not always, not always in the sunshine." She was not sure that he recognized her, yet he kept hold of her hand and would not let it go.

"No; you are not always in de sunshine, because de sunshine is not always here," observed Mrs. Tourtel in a reasonable voice, and with a side glance for the visitor.

"And I am not always here either," he murmured, half to himself. He took a firmer hold of his cousin's hand, and seemed to gain courage from the comfortable touch, for his thin voice changed from complaint to command. "You can go, Mrs. Tourtel," he said; "we don't require you here. We want to talk. You can go and set the tea-things in the next room. My cousin will stay and drink tea with me."

"Why, my cert'nly! of course Mrs. Pedvinn will stay tea. P'r'aps you'd like to put your bonnet off in the bedroom, first, ma'am?"

"No, no," he interposed testily, "she can lay it off here. No need for you to take her upstairs."

Servant and master exchanged a mute look; for the moment his old eyes were lighted up with the unforeseeing, unveiled triumph of a child; then they fell before hers. She turned, leaving the room with noiseless tread; although a large-built, ponderous woman, she walked with the softness of a cat.

"Sit down here close beside me," said Louis Renouf to his cousin; "I've something to tell you, something very important to tell you." He lowered his voice mysteriously, and glanced with apprehension at window and door, squeezing tight her hand. "I'm being robbed, my dear, robbed of everything I possess."

Mrs. Poidevin, already prepared for such a statement, answered complacently, "Oh, it must be your fancy, Cousin Louis. Mrs. Tourtel takes too good care of you for that."

"My dear," he whispered, "silver, linen, everything is going; even my fine white shirts from the shelves of the wardrobe. Yet everything belongs to poor John, who is in Australia, and who never writes to his father now. His last letter is ten years old — ten years old, my dear, and I don't need to read it over, for I know it by heart."

Tears of weakness gathered in his eyes, and began to trickle over on to his cheek.

"Oh, Cousin John will write soon, I'm

sure," said Mrs. Poidevin, with easy optimism; "I should n't wonder if he has made a fortune, and is on his way home to you at this moment."

"Ah, he will never make a fortune, my dear, he was always too fond of change. He had excellent capabilities, Louisa, but he was too fond of change. . . . And yet I often sit and pretend to myself he has made money, and is as proud to be with his poor old father as he used to be when quite a little lad. I plan out all we should do, and all he would say, and just how he would look . . . but that's only my make-believe; John will never make money, never. But I'd be glad if he would come back to the old home, though it were without a penny. For if he don't come soon, he'll find no home, and no welcome. . . . I raised all the money I could when he went away, and now, as you know, my dear, the house and land go to you and Pedvinn. . . . But I'd like my poor boy to have the silver and linen, and his mother's furniture and needlework to remember us by."

"Yes, cousin, and he will have them some day, but not for a great while yet, I hope."

Louis Renouf shook his head, with the immovable obstinacy of the very old or the very young.

"Louisa, mark my words, he will get nothing, nothing. Everything is going. They'll make away with the chairs and the tables next, with the very bed I lie on."

"Oh, Cousin Louis, you mustn't think such things," said Mrs. Poidevin, serenely; had not the poor old man accused her to the Tourtels of filching his mattress feathers?

"Ah, you don't believe me, my dear," said he, with a resignation which was pathetic; "but you'll remember my words when I am gone. Six dozen rat-tailed silver forks and spoons, with silver candlesticks, and tray, and snuffers. Besides odd pieces, and piles and piles of linen. Your cousin Betsy was a notable housekeeper, and everything she bought was of the very best. The large table-cloths were five guineas apiece, my dear, British money — five guineas apiece."

Louisa listened with perfect calmness and scant attention. Circumstances too comfortable, and a too abundant diet, had gradually undermined with her all perceptive and reflective powers. Though, of course, had the household effects been coming to her as well as the land, she would have felt more interest in them; but it is only human nature to contemplate the possible losses of others with equanimity.

"They must be handsome cloths, cousin," she said pleasantly; "I'm sure Pedvinn would never allow me half so much for mine."

At this moment there appeared, framed in the open window, the hideous vision of an animated gargoyle, with elf-locks of flaming red, and an intense malignancy of expression. With a finger dragging down the under eyelid of each eye, so that the eyeball seemed to bulge out — with a finger pulling back either corner of the wide mouth, so that it seemed to touch the ear — this repulsive apparition leered at the old man in blood-curdling fashion. Then, catching sight of Mrs. Poidevin, who sat dumbfounded, and with her "heart in her mouth," as she afterwards expressed it, the fingers dropped from the face, the features sprang back into position, and the gargoyle resolved itself into a buxom red-haired girl, who, bursting into a laugh, impudently stuck her tongue out at them before skipping away.

The old man had cowered down in his chair with his hands over his eyes; now he looked up. "I thought it was the old Judy," he said, "the old Judy she is always telling me about. But it's only Margot."

"And who is Margot, cousin?" inquired Louisa, still shaken from the surprise.

"She helps in the kitchen. But I don't like her. She pulls faces at me, and jumps out upon me from behind doors. And when the wind blows and the windows rattle she tells me about the old Judy from Jethou, who is sailing over the sea on a broomstick, to come and beat me to death. Do you know, my dear," he said piteously, "you'll think I'm very silly, but I'm afraid up here by myself all alone? Do not leave me, Louisa; stay with me, or take me back to town with you. Pedvinn would let me have a room in your house, I'm sure? And you wouldn't find me much trouble, and of course I would bring my own bed linen, you know."

"You had best take your tea first, sir," said Mrs. Tourtel from outside the window; she held scissors in her hand, and was busy trimming the roses. She offered no excuse for eavesdropping.

The meal was set out, Island fashion, with abundant cakes and sweets. Louisa saw in the silver tea-set another proof, if need be, of her cousin's unfounded suspicions. Mrs. Tourtel stood in the background, waiting. Renouf desired her to pack his things; he was going into town. "To be sure, sir," she said civilly, and remained where she stood. He brought a clenched hand down upon the table, so that the china rattled. "Are you master here, or am I?" he cried; "I am going down to my cousin Pedvinn's. To-morrow I shall send my notary to put seals on everything, and to take an inventory. For the future I shall live in town."

His senility had suddenly left him; he spoke with firmness; it was a flash-up of almost extinct fires. Louisa was astounded. Mrs. Tourtel looked at him steadily. Through the partition wall, Tourtel in the kitchen heard the raised voice, and followed his curiosity into the parlor. Margot followed him. Seen near, and with her features at rest, she appeared a plump, touzle-headed girl, in whose low forehead and loose-lipped mouth, crassness, cruelty, and sensuality were unmistakably expressed. Yet freckled cheek, rounded chin, and bare red mottled arms presented the beautiful curves of youth, and there was a certain sort of attractiveness about her not to be gainsaid.

"Since my servants refuse to pack what I require," said Renouf, with dignity, "I will do it myself. Come with me, Louisa."

At a sign from the housekeeper, Tourtel and Margot made way. Mrs. Poidevin would have followed her cousin, as the easiest thing to do — although she was confused by the old man's outbreak, and incapable of deciding what course she should take — when the deep vindictive baying of the dog ushered a new personage upon the scene.

This was an individual who made his appearance from the kitchen regions — a tall, thin man of about thirty years of age, with a pallid skin, a dark eye, and a heavy moustache. His shabby black coat and tie, with the cords and gaiters that clothed his legs, suggested a combination of sportsman and family practitioner. He wore a bowler hat, and was pulling off tan driving gloves as he advanced.

"Ah, my good! Doctor Owen, but dat's you?" said Mrs. Tourtel. "But we wants you here badly. Your patient is in one of his tantrums, and no one can't do nuddin wid him. He says he shall go right away into town. Wants to make up again wid Doctor Lelever for sure."

The new-comer and Mrs. Poidevin were examining each other with the curiosity one feels on first meeting a person long known by reputation or by sight. But now she turned to the housekeeper in surprise.

"Has my cousin quarrelled with his old friend Doctor Lelever?" she asked. "I've heard nothing of that."

"Ah, dis long time! He tought Doctor Lelever made too little of his megrims. He won't have nobody but Doctor Owen now. P'r'aps you know Doctor Owen, ma'am? Mrs. Pedvinn, Doctor; de master's cousin, come up to visit him."

Renouf was heard moving about overhead, opening presses, dragging boxes.

Owen hung up his hat, putting his gloves inside it. He rubbed his lean discolored hands lightly together, as a fly cleans its forelegs.

"Shall I just step up to him?" he said. "It may calm him, and distract his thoughts."

With soft nimbleness, in a moment he was upstairs. "So that's Doctor Owen?" observed Mrs. Poidevin with interest. "A splendid-looking gentleman! He must be very clever, I'm sure. Is he beginning to get a good practice yet?"

"Ah, bah! our people, as you know, ma'am, dey don't like no strangers, specially no Englishmen. He was very glad when Mr. Rennuf sent for him. . . . 'T was through Margot there. She got took bad one Saturday coming back from market from de heat or de squidge" (crowd), "and Doctor Owen he overtook her on the road in his gig, and druv her home. Den de master, he must have a talk with him, and so de next time he fancy hisself ill he send for Doctor Owen, and since den he don't care for Doctor Lelever no more at all."

"I ought to be getting off," remarked Mrs. Poidevin, remembering the hour at which the omnibus left Vauvert. "Had I better go up and bid Cousin Louis good-by?"

Mrs. Tourtel thought Margot should go and ask the Doctor's opinion first; but as Margot had already vanished, she went herself.

There was a longish pause, during which Mrs. Poidevin looked uneasily at Tourtel; he with restless, furtive eyes at her. Then the housekeeper reappeared, noiseless, cool, determined as ever.

"Mr. Rennuf is quiet now," she said; "de doctor have given him a soothing draught, and will stay to see how it axe. He tinks you better slip quietly away."

On this, Louisa Poidevin left Les Calais; but in spite of her easy superficiality, her unreasoning optimism, she took with her a sense of oppression. Cousin Louis's appeal rang in her ears: "Do not leave me; stay with me, or take me back with you. I am afraid up here, quite alone." And after all, though his fears were but the folly of old age, why, she asked herself, should he not come and stay with them in town if he wished to do so? She resolved to talk it over with Pedvinn; she thought she would arrange for him the little west room, being the furthest from the nurseries; and in planning out such vastly important trifles as to which easy-chair and which bedroom candlestick she would devote to his use, she forgot the old man himself and recovered her usual stolid jocundity.

When Owen had entered the bedroom, he had found Renouf standing over an open portmanteau, into which he was placing hurriedly whatever caught his eye or took his fancy from the surrounding tables. His hand trembled from eagerness, his pale old face was flushed with excitement and hope. Owen, going straight up to him, put his two hands on his shoulders, and, without uttering a word, gently forced him backwards into a chair. Then he sat down in front of him, so close that their knees touched, and fixing his strong eyes on Renouf's wavering ones, and stroking with his finger-tips the muscles behind the ears, he threw him immediately into an hypnotic trance.

"You want to stay here, don't you?" said Owen, emphatically.

"I want to stay here," repeated the old man through gray lips. His face was become the color of ashes, his hands were cold to the sight.

"You want your cousin to go away and not disturb you any more? Answer — answer me."

"I want my cousin to go away," Renouf murmured, but in his staring, fading eye were traces of the struggle tearing him within.

Owen pressed down the eyelids, made another pass before the face, and rose on his long legs with a sardonic grin. Margot, leaning across a corner of the bed, had watched him with breathless interest.

"I b'lieve you're de Evil One himself," she said, admiringly.

Owen pinched her smooth chin between his tobacco-stained thumb and fingers.

"Pooh! nothing but a trick I learned in Paris," said he; "it's very convenient to be able to put a person to sleep now and again."

"Could you put any one to sleep?"

"Any one I wanted to."

"Do it to me then," she begged him.

"What use, my girl? Don't you do all I wish without?"

She grimaced, and picked at the bed-quilt laughing, then rose and stood in front of him, her round red arms clasped behind her head. But he only glanced at her with professional interest.

"You should get married, my dear, without delay. Pierre would be ready enough, no doubt?"

"Bah! Pierre or annuder — if I brought a weddin' portion. You don't tink to provide me wid one, I s'pose?"

"You know that I can't. But why don't you get it from the Tourtels? You've earned it before this, I dare swear."

It was now that the housekeeper came up, and took down to Louisa Poidevin the message given above. But first she was detained by Owen, to assist him in getting his patient into bed.

The old man woke up during the process, very peevish, very determined to get to town. "Well, you can't go till to-morrow den," said Mrs. Tourtel; "your cousin has gone home, an' now you've got to go to sleep, so be quiet." She dropped all semblance of respect in her tones. "Come, lie down!" she said, sharply, "or I'll send Margot to tickle your feet." He shivered and whimpered into silence beneath the clothes.

"Margot tells him 'bout witches, an' ogres, and scrapels her fingures 'long de wall, till he tinks dere goin' to fly 'way wid him," she explained to Owen in an aside. "Oh, I know Margot," he answered laconically, and thought, 'May I never lie helpless within reach of such fingers as hers.'"

He took a step, and stumbled over a portmanteau gaping open at his feet. "Put your mischievous paws to some use," he told the girl, "and clear these things away from the floor;" then, remembering his rival Le Lièvre, "if the old fool had really got away to town, it would have been a nice day's work for us all," he added.

Downstairs he joined the Tourtels in the kitchen, a room situated behind a living room on the left, with low green glass windows, rafters and woodwork, smoke-browned with the fires of a dozen generations. In the wooden racks over by the chimney hung flitches of home-cured bacon, and the kettle was suspended by three chains over the centre of the wide hearth, where glowed and crackled an armful of sticks. So dark was the room, in spite of the daylight outside, that two candles were set in the centre of the table, enclosing in their circles of yellow light the pale face and silver hair of the housekeeper and Tourtel's rugged head and weather-beaten countenance.

He had glasses ready, and a bottle of the cheap brandy for which the Island is famous. "You'll take a drop of something, eh, doctor?" he said, as Owen seated himself on the "jonquière," a padded settle — green baize covered, to replace the primitive rushes — fitted on one side of the hearth. He stretched his long legs into the light, and for a moment considered moodily the old gaiters and cobbled boots. "You've seen to the horse?" he asked Tourtel.

"My, cert'nly; he's in de stable dis hour back, an' I've given him a feed. I tought maybe you'd make a night of it."

"I may as well for all the work I have to do," said Owen, with sourness; "a damned little Island this for doctors. Nothing ever the matter with any one except the 'creeps,' and those who have it, spend their last penny in making it worse."

"Dere's as much illness here as anywhere," said Tourtel, defending the reputation of his native soil, "if once you gets among de right class, among de people as has de time an' de money to make derselves ill. But if you go foolin' roun' wid de paysans, what can you expeck'? We workin' folks can't afford to lay up an' buy ourselves doctors' stuff."

"And how am I to get among the right class?" retorted Owen, sucking the ends of his moustache into his mouth and chewing them savagely. "A more confounded set of stuck-up, beggarly aristocrats I never met than your people here." His discontented eye rested on Mrs. Tourtel. "That Mrs. Pedvinn is the wife of Pedvinn the Jurat, I suppose?"

"Yes, de Pedvinns of Rohais."

"Good people," said Owen, thoughtfully; "in with the de Câterelles, and the Dadderney" (d'Aldenos) "set. Are there children?"

"Tree."

POOR COUSIN LOUIS.

He took a drink of the spirit and water; his bad temper passed. Margot came in from upstairs.

"De marster sleeps as dough he'd never wake again," she announced, flinging herself into the chair nearest Owen.

"It's 'bout time he did," Tourtel growled.

"I should have thought it more to your interest to keep him alive?" Owen inquired. "A good place, surely?"

"A good place if you like to call it so," the wife answered him; "but what, if he go to town, as he say to-night? and what, if he send de notary, to put de scellés here? — den he take up again wid Dr. Lelever, dat's certain." And Tourtel added in his surly key, "Anyway, I've been workin' here dese tirty years now, and dat's 'bout enough."

"In fact, when the orange is sucked, you throw away the peel? But are you quite sure it is sucked dry?"

"De house an' de lan' go to de Pedvinns, an' all de money die too, for de little he had left when young John went 'crost de seas, he sunk in a 'nuity. Dere's nuddin' but de lining, an' plate, an' such like, as goes to de son."

"And what he finds of that, I expect, will

scarcely add to his impedimenta," said Owen, grinning. He thought, "The old man is well known in the Island, the name of his medical attendant would get mentioned in the papers at least; just as well Lelever should not have the advertisement." Besides, there were the Poidevins.

"You might say a good word for me to Mrs. Pedvinn," he said aloud. "I live nearer to Rohais than Lelever does, and, with young children, she might be glad to have some one at hand."

"You may be sure you won't never find me ungrateful, sir," answered the housekeeper; and Owen, shading his eyes with his hand, sat pondering over the use of this word "ungrateful," with its faint yet perceptible emphasis.

Margot, meanwhile, laid the supper; the remains of a rabbit-pie, a big "pinclos," or spider crab, with thin, red knotted legs, spreading far over the edges of the dish, the apple-gôche, hot from the oven, cider, and the now half-empty bottle of brandy. The four sat down and fell to. Margot was in boisterous spirits; everything she said or did was meant to attract Owen's attention. Her cheeks flamed with excitement; she wanted his eyes to be perpetually upon her. But Owen's interest in her had long ceased. To-night, while eating heartily, he was absorbed in his ruling passion: to get on in the world, to make money, to be admitted into Island society. Behind the pallid, impenetrable mask, which always enraged yet intimidated Margot, he plotted incessantly, schemed, combined, weighed this and that, studied his prospects from every point of view.

Supper over, he lighted his meerschaum; Tourtel produced a short clay, and the bottle was passed between them. The women left them together, and for ten, twenty minutes, there was complete silence in the room. Tourtel let his pipe go out, and rapped it down brusquely upon the table.

"It must come to an end," he said, with suppressed ferocity; "are we eider to spen' de whole of our lives here, or else be turned off at de eleventh hour after sufferin' all de heat an' burden of de day? It's onreasonable. An' dere's de cottage at Cottu standin' empty, an' me havin' to pay a man to look after de tomato houses, when I could get fifty per cent more by lookin' after dem myself. . . . An' what profit is such a sickly, shiftless life as dat?

My good! dere's not a man, woman, or chile in de Islan's as will shed a tear when he goes, an' dere's some, I tells you, as have suffered from his whimsies dese tirty years, as will rejoice. Why, his wife was dead already when we come here, an' his on'y son, a dirty, drunken, lazy vaurien too, has never been near him for fifteen years, nor written neider. Dead most likely, in foreign parts. . . . An' what's he want to stay for, contraryin' an' thwartin' dem as have sweated an' labored, an' now, please de good God, wan's to sit 'neath de shadow of dere own fig-tree for de short time dat remains to dem? . . . An' what do we get for stayin'? Forty pound, Island money, between de two of us, an' de little I makes from de flowers, an' poultry, an' such like. An' what do we do for it? Bake, an' wash, an' clean, an' cook, an' keep de garden in order, an' nuss him in all his tantrums. . . . If we was even on his testament, I'd say nuddin. But everything goes to Pedvinns, an' de son John, an' de little bit of income dies wid him. I tell you 't is 'bout time dis came to an end."

Owen recognized that Destiny asked no sin more heinous from him than silence, perhaps concealment; the chestnuts would reach him without risk of burning his hand. "It's time," said he, "I thought of going home. Get your lantern, and I'll help you with the trap. But first, I'll just run up and have another look at Mr. Rennuf."

For the last time the five personages of this obscure little tragedy found themselves together in the bedroom, now lighted by a small lamp which stood on the wash-hand stand. Owen, who had to stoop to enter the door, could have touched the low-pitched ceiling with his hand. The bed, with its slender pillars, supporting a canopy of faded damask, took up the greater part of the room. There was a fluted headpiece of the damask, and long curtains of the same material, looped up, on either side of the pillows. Sunken in these lay the head of the old man, crowned with a cotton nightcap, the eyes closed, the skin drawn tight over the skull, the outline of the attenuated form indistinguishable beneath the clothes. The arms lay outside the counterpane, straight down on either side; and the mechanical playing movement of the fingers showed he was not asleep. Margot and Mrs. Tourtel watched them from the bed's foot. Their gigantic shadows, thrown forward by the lamp, stretched up the opposite wall, and covered half the ceiling. The old-fashioned mahogany furniture, with its fillets of paler wood, drawn in ovals, upon the doors of the presses, their centrepieces of fruit and flowers, shone out here and there with reflected light; and the looking-glass, swung on corkscrew mahogany pillars between the damask window curtains, gleamed lake-like amidst the gloom.

Owen and Tourtel joined the women at the bed-foot. Though each was absorbed entirely in his own egotisms, all were animated by the same secret desire. Yet, to the feeling heart, there was something unspeakably pleading in the sight of the old man lying there, in his helplessness, in the very room, on the very bed, which had seen his wedding-night forty years before; where, as a much-wished-for and welcomed infant, he had opened his eyes to the light more than seventy years since. He had been helpless then as now, but then the child had been held to loving hearts, loving fingers had tended him, a young and loving mother lay beside him, the circumference of all his tiny world, as he was the core and centre of all of hers. And from being that exquisite, well-beloved little child, he had passed thoughtlessly, hopefully, despairfully, wearily, through all the stages of life, until he had come to this — a poor old, feeble, helpless, worn-out man, lying there where he had been born, but with all those who had loved him carried long ago to the grave; with the few who might have protected him still, his son, his cousin, his old friend Le Lièvre, as powerless to save him as the silent dead.

Renouf opened his eyes, looked in turn at the four faces before him, and read as much pity in them as in masks of stone. He turned himself to the pillow again and to his miserable thoughts.

Owen took out his watch, went round to count the pulse, and in the hush the tick of the big silver timepiece could be heard.

"There is extreme weakness," came his quiet verdict.

"Sinking?" whispered Tourtel loudly.

"No; care and constant nourishment are all that are required; strong beef-tea, port-wine jelly, cream beaten up with a little brandy at short intervals, every hour say. And of course no excitement; nothing to irritate or alarm him" (Owen's eye met Margot's); "absolute quiet and rest." He came back to the foot of the bed and spoke in a lower tone. "It's just one of the usual cases of senile decay," said he, "which I observe every one comes to here in the Islands (unless he has previously killed himself by drink), the results of breeding in. But Mr. Rennuf may last months, years, longer. In fact, if you follow out my directions there is every probability that he will."

Tourtel and his wife shifted their gaze from Owen to look into each other's eyes; Margot's loose mouth lapsed into a smile. Owen felt cold water running down his back. The atmosphere of the room seemed to stifle him; reminiscences of his student days crowded on him. The horror of an unperverted mind at its first spectacle of cruelty again seized hold of him, vivid as though no twelve benumbing years were wedged between. At all costs he must get out into the open air.

He turned to go. Louis Renouf opened his eyes, followed the form making its way to the door, and understood. "You won't leave me, doctor? surely you won't leave me?" came the last words of piercing entreaty.

The man felt his nerve going all to pieces.

"Come, come, my good sir, do you think I am going to stay here all night?" he answered brutally. . . . Outside, Tourtel touched his sleeve. "And suppose your directions are not carried out?" asked he in his thick whisper.

Owen gave no spoken answer, but Tourtel was satisfied. "I'll come an' put the horse in," he said, leading the way through the kitchen to the stables. Owen drove off with a parting curse, and cut with the whip because the horse slipped upon the stones. A long ray of light from Tourtel's lantern followed him down the lane. When he turned out on to the high-road to St. Gilles he reined in a moment, to look back at Les Calais. This is the one point from which a portion of the house is visible, and he could see the lighted window of the old man's bedroom plainly through the trees.

What was happening there? he asked himself; and the Tourtels' cupidity and callousness, Margot's coarse cruel tricks, rose before him with appalling distinctness. Yet the price was in his hand, the first step of the ladder gained; he saw himself to-morrow, perhaps in the drawing-room of Rohais, paying the necessary visit of intimation and condolence. He felt he had already won Mrs. Poidevin's favor. Among women, always poor physiognomists, he knew he passed for a handsome man; among the Islanders, the assurance of his address would pass for good breeding; all he had lacked hitherto was the opportunity to shine. This, his acquaintance with Mrs. Poidevin would secure him. And he had trampled on his conscience so often before, it had now little elasticity left. Just an extra glass of brandy to-morrow, and to-day would be as securely laid as those other episodes of his past.

While he watched, some one shifted the lamp . . . a woman's shadow was thrown upon the white blind . . . it wavered, grew monstrous, and spread, until the whole window was shrouded in gloom. . . . Owen put the horse into a gallop . . . and from up at Les Calais, the long-drawn, melancholy howling of the dog filled with forebodings the silent night.

THE PLEASURE-PILGRIM.

THE PLEASURE-PILGRIM.

I.

CAMPBELL was on his way to Schloss Altenau, for a second quiet season with his work. He had spent three profitable months there a year ago, and he was hoping now for a repetition of that good fortune. His thoughts outran the train; and long before his arrival at the Hamelin railway station, he was enjoying his welcome by the Ritterhausens, was revelling in the ease and comfort of the old castle, and was contrasting the pleasures of his home-coming — for he looked upon Schloss Altenau as a sort of temporary home — with his recent cheerless experiences of lodging-houses in London, hotels in Berlin, and strange indifferent faces everywhere. He thought with especial satisfaction of the Maynes, and of the good talks Mayne and he would have together, late at night, before the great fire in the hall, after the rest of the household had gone to bed.

He blessed the adverse circumstances which had turned Schloss Altenau into a boarding-house, and had reduced the Freiherr Ritterhausen to eke out his shrunken revenues by the reception, as paying guests, of English and American pleasure-pilgrims.

He rubbed the blurred window-pane with the fringed end of the strap hanging from it, and, in the snow-covered landscape reeling towards him, began to recognize objects that were familiar. Hamelin could not be far off. . . . In another ten minutes the train came to a standstill.

He stepped down with a sense of relief from the overheated atmosphere of his compartment into the cold bright February afternoon, and saw through the open station doors one of the Ritterhausen carriages awaiting him, with Gottlieb in his second-best livery on the box. Gottlieb showed every reasonable consideration for the Baron's boarders, but had various methods of marking his sense of the immense abyss separating them from the family. The use of his second-best livery was one of these methods. Nevertheless, he turned a friendly German eye up to Campbell, and in response to his cordial "Guten Tag, Gottlieb.

Wie geht's? Und die Herrschaften?" expressed his pleasure at seeing the young man back again.

While Campbell stood at the top of the steps that led down to the carriage and the Platz, looking after the collection of his luggage and its bestowal by Gottlieb's side, he became aware of two persons, ladies, advancing towards him from the direction of the Wartsaal. It was surprising to see any one at any time in Hamelin station. It was still more surprising when one of these ladies addressed him by name.

"You are Mr. Campbell, are you not?" she said. "We have been waiting for you to go back in the carriage together. When we found this morning that there was only half an hour between your train and ours, I told the Baroness it would be perfectly absurd to send to the station twice. I hope you won't mind our company?"

The first impression Campbell received was of the magnificent apparel of the lady before him; it would have been noticeable in Paris or Vienna — it was extravagant here. Next, he perceived that the face beneath the upstanding feathers and the curving hat-brim was that of

so very young a girl as to make the furs and
velvets seem more incongruous still. But the
sense of incongruity vanished with the intonation of her first phrase, which told him she
was an American. He had no standards for
American conduct. It was clear that the
speaker and her companion were inmates of
the Schloss.

He bowed, and murmured the pleasure he
did not feel. A true Briton, he was intolerably shy; and his heart sank at the prospect of a three-mile drive with two strangers
who evidently had the advantage of knowing
all about him, while he was in ignorance of
their very names. As he took his place opposite to them in the carriage, he unconsciously
assumed a cold, blank stare, pulling nervously
at his moustache, as was his habit in moments
of discomposure. Had his companions been
British also, the ordeal of the drive must have
been a terrible one; but these young American
ladies showed no sense of embarrassment
whatever.

"We've just come back from Hanover," said
the girl who had already spoken to him. "I
go over once a week for a singing lesson, and
my little sister comes along to take care of me."

She turned a narrow, smiling glance from Campbell to her little sister, and then back to Campbell again. She had red hair, freckles on her nose, and the most singular eyes he had ever seen; slit-like eyes, set obliquely in her head, Chinese fashion.

"Yes, Lulie requires a great deal of taking care of," assented the little sister sedately, though the way in which she said this seemed to imply something less simple than the words themselves. The speaker bore no resemblance to Lulie. She was smaller, thinner, paler. Her features were straight, a trifle peaked; her skin sallow; her hair of a nondescript brown. She was much less gorgeously dressed. There was even a suggestion of shabbiness in her attire, though sundry isolated details of it were handsome too. She was also much less young; or so, at any rate, Campbell began by pronouncing her. Yet presently he wavered. She had a face that defied you to fix her age. Campbell never fixed it to his own satisfaction, but veered in the course of that drive (as he was destined to do during the next few weeks) from point to point up and down the scale from eighteen to thirty-five. She wore a spotted veil, and beneath it a pince-nez, the lenses of which did something to temper the immense amount of humorous meaning which lurked in her gaze. When her pale prominent eyes met Campbell's, it seemed to the young man that they were full of eagerness to add something at his expense to the stores of information they had already garnered up. They chilled him with misgivings; there was more comfort to be found in her sister's shifting, red-brown glances.

"Hanover is a long way to go for lessons," he observed, forcing himself to be conversational. "I used to go there myself about once a week, when I first came to Schloss Altenau, for tobacco, or note-paper, or to get my hair cut. But later on I did without, or contented myself with what Hamelin, or even the village, could offer me."

"Nannie and I," said the young girl, "meant to stay only a week at Altenau, on our way to Hanover, where we were going to pass the winter; but the Castle is just too lovely for anything." She raised her eyelids the least little bit as she looked at him, and such a warm and friendly gaze shot out, that Campbell was suddenly thrilled. Was she pretty, after all? He glanced at Nannie; she, at least, was indubitably plain. "It's the very first time we've ever stayed in a castle," Lulie went on; "and we're going to remain right along now, until we go home in the spring. Just imagine living in a house with a real moat, and a drawbridge, and a Rittersaal, and suits of armor that have been actually worn in battle! And oh, that delightful iron collar and chain! You remember it, Mr. Campbell? It hangs right close to the gateway on the courtyard side. And you know, in old days the Ritterhausens used it for the punishment of their serfs. There are horrible stories connected with it. Mr. Mayne can tell you them. But just think of being chained up there like a dog! So wonderfully picturesque."

"For the spectator perhaps," said Campbell, smiling. "I doubt if the victim appreciated the picturesque aspect of the case."

With this Lulie disagreed. "Oh, I think he must have been interested," she said. "It must have made him feel so absolutely part and parcel of the Middle Ages. I persuaded Mr. Mayne to fix the collar round my neck the other day; and though it was very uncomfortable, and I had to stand on tiptoe, it seemed to me that all at once the courtyard was filled with knights in armor, and crusaders, and palmers, and things; and there were flags flying and trumpets sounding; and all the dead and gone Ritterhausens had come down from their picture-frames, and were walking about in brocaded gowns and lace ruffles."

"It seemed to require a good deal of persuasion to get Mr. Mayne to unfix the collar again," said the little sister. "How at last did you manage it?"

But Lulie replied irrelevantly: "And the Ritterhausens are such perfectly lovely people, are n't they, Mr. Campbell? The old Baron is a perfect dear. He has such a grand manner. When he kisses my hand I feel nothing less than a princess. And the Baroness is such a funny, busy, delicious little round ball of a thing. And she 's always playing bagatelle, is n't she? Or else cutting up skeins of wool for carpet-making." She meditated a moment. "Some people always *are* cutting things up in order to join them together again," she announced, in her fresh drawling young voice.

"And some people cut things up, and leave other people to do the reparation," commented the little sister, enigmatically.

And meantime the carriage had been rattling

over the cobble-paved streets of the quaint mediæval town, where the houses stand so near together that you may shake hands with your opposite neighbor; where allegorical figures, strange birds and beasts, are carved and painted over the windows and doors; and where to every distant sound you lean your ear to catch the fairy music of the Pied Piper, and at every street corner you look to see his tatterdemalion form with the frolicking children at his heels.

Then the Weser bridge was crossed, beneath which the ice-floes jostled and ground themselves together, as they forced their way down the river; and the carriage was rolling smoothly along country roads, between vacant snow-decked fields.

Campbell's embarrassment began to wear off. Now that he was getting accustomed to the girls, he found neither of them awe-inspiring. The red-haired one had a simple childlike manner that was charming. Her strange little face, with its piquant irregularity of line, its warmth of color, began to please him. What though her hair was red, the uncurled wisp which strayed across her white forehead was soft and alluring; he could see soft masses of it tucked up beneath her hat-brim as she turned her head. When she suddenly lifted her red-brown lashes, those queer eyes of hers had a velvety softness too. Decidedly, she struck him as being pretty — in a peculiar way. He felt an immense accession of interest in her. It seemed to him that he was the discoverer of her possibilities. He did not doubt that the rest of the world called her plain, or at least odd-looking. He, at first, had only seen the freckles on her nose, her oblique-set eyes. He wondered now what she thought of herself, how she appeared to Nannie. Probably as a very ordinary little girl; sisters stand too close to see each other's qualities. She was too young to have had much opportunity of hearing flattering truths from strangers; and, besides, the average stranger would see nothing in her to call for flattering truths. Her charm was something subtle, out-of-the-common, in defiance of all known rules of beauty. Campbell saw superiority in himself for recognizing it, for formulating it; and he was not displeased to be aware that it would always remain caviare to the multitude.

The carriage had driven through the squalid village of Dürrendorf, had passed the great Ritterhausen barns and farm-buildings, on the

THE PLEASURE-PILGRIM.

tie-beams of which are carved Bible texts in old German; had turned in at the wide-open gates of Schloss Altenau, where Gottlieb always whipped up his horses to a fast trot. Full of feeling both for the pocket and the dignity of the Ritterhausens, he would not use up his beasts in unnecessary fast driving. But it was to the credit of the family that he should reach the Castle in fine style. And so he thundered across the drawbridge, and through the great archway pierced in the north wing, and over the stones of the cobbled courtyard, to pull up before the door of the hall, with much clattering of hoofs and a final elaborate whip-flourish.

II.

"I'M jolly glad to have you back," Mayne said, that same evening, when, the rest of the boarders having retired to their rooms, he and Campbell were lingering over the hall-fire for a talk and smoke. "I've missed you awfully, old chap, and the good times we used to have here. I've often meant to write to you, but you know how one shoves off letter-writing day after day, till at last one is too ashamed of one's indolence to write at all. But tell me — you had a pleasant drive from Hamelin? What do you think of our young ladies?"

"Those American girls? But they 're charming," said Campbell, with enthusiasm. "The red-haired one is particularly charming."

At this Mayne laughed so strangely that Campbell questioned him in surprise. "Is n't she charming?"

"My dear chap," Mayne told him, "the red-haired one, as you call her, is the most remarkably charming young person I 've ever met or read of. We 've had a good many American girls here before now — you remember the good old Choate family, of course — they were here in your time, I think? — but we 've never had anything like this Miss Lulie Thayer. She is something altogether unique."

Campbell was struck with the name. "Lulie — Lulie Thayer," he repeated. "How pretty it is!" And, full of his great discovery, he felt he must confide it to Mayne, at least. "Do you know," he went on, "*she* is really very pretty too? I did n't think so at first, but after a bit I discovered that she is positively quite pretty — in an odd sort of way."

Mayne laughed again. "Pretty, pretty!" he echoed in derision. "Why, *lieber Gott im Himmel*, where are your eyes? Pretty! The girl is beautiful, gorgeously beautiful; every trait, every tint, is in complete, in absolute harmony with the whole. But the truth is, of course, we've all grown accustomed to the obvious, the commonplace; to violent contrasts; blue eyes, black eyebrows, yellow hair; the things that shout for recognition. You speak of Miss Thayer's hair as red. What other color would you have, with that warm, creamy skin? And then, what a red it is! It looks as though it had been steeped in red wine."

"Ah, what a good description!" said Campbell, appreciatively. "That's just it — steeped in red wine."

"Though it's not so much her beauty," Mayne continued. "After all, one has met beautiful women before now. It's her wonderful generosity, her complaisance. She doesn't keep her good things to herself. She doesn't condemn you to admire from a distance."

"How do you mean?" Campbell asked, surprised again.

"Why, she's the most egregious little flirt

I've ever met. And yet, she's not exactly a flirt, either. I mean she doesn't flirt in the ordinary way. She doesn't talk much, or laugh, or apparently make the least claims on masculine attention. And so all the women like her. I don't believe there's one, except my wife, who has an inkling as to her true character. The Baroness, as you know, never observes anything. *Seigneur Dieu!* if she knew the things I could tell her about Miss Lulie! For I've had opportunities of studying her. You see, I'm a married man, and not in my first youth, and the looker-on generally gets the best view of the game. But you, who are young and charming and already famous — we've had your book here, by the by, and there's good stuff in it — you're going to have no end of pleasant experiences. I can see she means to add you to her ninety-and-nine other spoils; I saw it from the way she looked at you at dinner. She always begins with those velvety red-brown glances. She began that way with March and Prendergast and Willie Anson, and all the men we've had here since her arrival. The next thing she'll do will be to press your hand under the tablecloth."

"Oh, come, Mayne, you're joking," cried Campbell, a little brusquely. He thought such jokes in bad taste. He had a high ideal of Woman, an immense respect for her; he could not endure to hear her belittled, even in jest. "Miss Thayer is refined and charming. No girl of her class would do such things."

"But what is her class? Who knows anything about her? All we know is that she and her uncanny little friend — her little sister, as she calls her, though they're no more sisters than you and I are — they're not even related — all we know is, that she and Miss Dodge (that's the little sister's name) arrived here one memorable day last October from the Kronprinz Hotel at Waldeck-Pyrmont. By the by, it was the Choates, I believe, who told her of the Castle — hotel acquaintances — you know how travelling Americans always cotton to each other. And we've picked up a few little auto and biographical notes from her and Miss Dodge since. *Zum Beispiel*, she's got a rich father somewhere away back in Michigan, who supplies her with all the money she wants. And she's been travelling about since last May: Paris, Vienna, the Rhine, Düsseldorf, and so on here. She must have had some rich experiences, by Jove, for she's done everything. Cycled in Paris: you should see her in her cycling costume, she wears it when the Baron takes her out shooting — she's an admirable shot by the way, an accomplishment learned, I suppose, from some American cow-boy; then in Berlin she did a month's hospital nursing; and now she's studying the higher branches of the Terpsichorean art. You know she was in Hanover to-day. Did she tell you what she went for?"

"To take a singing lesson," said Campbell, remembering the reason she had given.

"A singing lesson! Do you sing with your legs? A dancing lesson, *mein lieber.* A dancing lesson from the ballet-master of the Hof Theater. She could deposit a kiss on your forehead with her foot, I don't doubt. I must ask her if she can do the *grand écart* yet." And when Campbell, in astonishment, wondered why on earth she should wish to learn such things, "Oh, to extend her opportunities," Mayne explained, "and to acquire fresh sensations. She's an adventuress. Yes, an adventuress, but an end-of-the-century one. She does n't travel for profit, but for pleasure. She has no desire to swindle her neighbor, but to amuse herself. And she's clever; she's read a good deal; she knows how to apply her reading to practical life. Thus, she's learned from Herrick not to be coy; and from Shakespeare that sweet-and-twenty is the time for kissing and being kissed. She honors her masters in the observance. She was not in the least abashed when, one day, I suddenly came upon her teaching that damned idiot, young Anson, two new ways of kissing."

Campbell's impressions of the girl were readjusting themselves completely, but for the moment he was unconscious of the change. He only knew that he was partly angry, partly incredulous, and inclined to believe that Mayne was chaffing him.

"But Miss Dodge," he objected, "the little sister, she is older; old enough to look after her friend. Surely she could not allow a young girl placed in her charge to behave in such a way —"

"Oh, that little Dodge girl," said Mayne contemptuously. "Miss Thayer pays the whole shot, I understand, and Miss Dodge plays gooseberry, sheep-dog, jackal, what you will. She finds her reward in the other's cast-off finery. The silk blouse she was wearing to-night, I've good reason for remembering, belonged to Miss Lulie. For, during a brief season, I must tell you, my young lady had the caprice to show attentions to your humble servant. I suppose my being a married man lent me a factitious fascination. But I did n't see it. That kind of girl does n't appeal to me. So she employed Miss Dodge to do a little active canvassing. It was really too funny; I was coming in one day after a walk in the woods; my wife was trimming bonnets, or had neuralgia, or something. Anyhow, I was alone, and Miss Dodge contrived to waylay me in the middle of the courtyard. 'Don't you find it vurry dull walking all by yourself?' she asked me; and then, blinking up in her strange little short-sighted way — she's really the weirdest little creature — 'Why don't you make love to Lulie?' she said; 'you'd find her vurry charming.' It took me a minute or two to recover presence of mind enough to ask her whether Miss Thayer had commissioned her to tell me so. She looked at me with that cryptic smile of hers; 'She'd like you to do so, I'm sure,' she finally remarked, and pirouetted away. Though it did n't come off, owing to my bashfulness, it was then that Miss Dodge appropriated the silk 'waist;' and Providence, taking pity on Miss Thayer's forced inactivity, sent along March, a young fellow reading for the army, with whom she had great doings. She fooled him to the top of his bent; sat on his knee; gave him a lock of her hair, which, having no scissors handy, she burned off with a cigarette taken from his mouth; and got him to offer her marriage. Then she turned round and laughed in his face, and took up with a Dr. Weber, a cousin of the Baron's, under the other man's very eyes. You never saw anything like the unblushing coolness with which she would permit March to catch her in Weber's arms."

"Come," Campbell protested again, "aren't you drawing it rather strong?"

"On the contrary, I'm drawing it mild, as you'll discover presently for yourself; and then you'll thank me for forewarning you. For she makes love — desperate love, mind you — to every man she meets. And goodness knows how many she hasn't met in the course of her career, which began presumably at the age of ten, in some 'Amur'can' hotel or watering-place. Look at this." Mayne fetched an alpenstock from a corner of the hall; it was decorated with a long succession of names, which, ribbon-like, were twisted round and round it, carved in the wood. "Read them," insisted Mayne, putting the stick in Campbell's hands. "You'll see they're not the names of the peaks she has climbed, or the towns she has passed through; they're the names of the men she has fooled. And there's room for more; there's still a good deal of space, as you see. There's room for yours."

Campbell glanced down the alpenstock — reading here a name, there an initial, or just a date — and jerked it impatiently from him on to a couch. He wished with all his heart that Mayne would stop, would talk of something else, would let him get away. The young girl had interested him so much; he had felt himself so drawn towards her; he had thought her so fresh, so innocent. But Mayne, on the contrary, was warming to his subject, was enchanted to have some one to listen to his stories, to discuss his theories, to share his cynical amusement.

"I don't think, mind you," he said, "that she is a bit interested herself in the men she flirts with. I don't think she gets any of the usual sensations from it, you know. My theory is, she does it for mere devilry, for a laugh. Or, and this is another theory, she is actuated by some idea of retribution. Perhaps some woman she was fond of — her mother even — who knows? — was badly treated at the hands of a man. Perhaps this girl has constituted herself the Nemesis for her sex, and goes about seeing how many masculine hearts she can break, by way of revenge. Or can it be that she is simply the newest development of the New Woman — she who in England preaches and bores you, and in America practises and pleases? Yes, I believe she's the American edition, and so new that she hasn't yet found her way into fiction. She's the pioneer of the army coming out of the West, that's going to destroy the existing scheme of things and rebuild it nearer to the heart's desire."

"Oh, damn it all, Mayne," cried Campbell, rising abruptly, "why not say at once that she's a wanton, and have done with it? Who wants to hear your rotten theories?" And he lighted his candle without another word, and went off to bed.

III.

It was four o'clock, and the Baron's boarders were drinking their afternoon coffee, drawn up in a semicircle round the hall fire. All but Campbell, who had carried his cup away to a side-table, and, with a book open beside him, appeared to be reading assiduously. In reality he could not follow a line of what he read; he could not keep his thoughts from Miss Thayer. What Mayne had told him was germinating in his mind. Knowing his friend as he did, he could not on reflection doubt his word. In spite of much superficial cynicism, Mayne was incapable of speaking lightly of any young girl without good cause. It now seemed to Campbell that, instead of exaggerating the case, Mayne had probably understated it. He asked himself with horror, what had this girl not already known, seen, permitted? When now and again his eyes travelled over perforce to where she sat, her red head leaning against Miss Dodge's knee, and seeming to attract to, and concentrate upon itself all the glow of the fire, his forehead set itself in frowns, and he returned to his book with an increased sense of irritation.

"I'm just sizzling up, Nannie," Miss Thayer presently complained, in her child-like, drawling little way; "this fire is too hot for anything." She rose and shook straight her loose tea-gown, a marvellous plush and lace garment created in Paris, which would have accused a duchess of wilful extravagance. She stood smiling round a moment, pulling on and off with her right hand a big diamond ring which decorated the left. At the sound of her voice Campbell had looked up, and his cold, unfriendly eyes encountered hers. He glanced rapidly past her, then back to his book. But she, undeterred, with a charming sinuous movement and a frou-frou of trailing silks, crossed over towards him. She slipped into an empty chair next his.

"I'm going to do you the honor of sitting beside you, Mr. Campbell," she said sweetly.

"It's an honor I've done nothing whatever to merit," he answered, without looking at her, and turned a page.

"The right retort," she approved; "but you might have said it a little more cordially."

"I don't feel cordial."

"But why not? What has happened? Yesterday you were so nice."

"Ah, a good deal of water has run under the bridge since yesterday."

"But still the river remains as full," she told him smiling, "and still the sky is as blue. The thermometer has even risen six degrees."

"What did you go into Hanover for yesterday?" Campbell suddenly asked her.

She flashed him a comprehending glance from half-shut eyes. "I think men gossip a great deal more than women," she observed, "and they don't understand things either. They try to make all life suit their own preconceived theories. And why, after all, should I not wish to learn dancing thoroughly? There's no harm in that."

"Only, why call it singing?" Campbell inquired.

Miss Thayer smiled. "Truth is so uninteresting!" she said, and paused. "Except in books. One likes it there. And I wanted to tell you, I think your books perfectly lovely. I know them, most all. I've read them away home. They're very much thought of in America. Only last night I was saying to Nannie how glad I am to have met you, for I think we're going to be great friends, are n't we, Mr. Campbell? At least, I hope so, for you can do me so much good, if you will. Your books always make me feel real good; but you yourself can help me much more."

She looked up at him with one of her warm, narrow red-brown glances, which yesterday would have thrilled his blood, and to-day merely stirred it to anger.

"You overestimate my abilities," he said coldly; "and, on the whole, I fear you will find writers a very disappointing race. You see, they put their best into their books. So not to disillusion you too rapidly " — he rose — " will you excuse me? I have some work to do." And he left her sitting there alone.

But he did no work when he got to his room. Whether Lulie Thayer was actually present or not, it seemed that her influence was equally disturbing to him. His mind was full of her: of her singular eyes, her quaint intonation, her sweet, seductive praise. Twenty-four hours ago such praise would have been delightful to him: what young author is proof against appreciation of his books? Now Campbell simply told himself that she laid the butter on too thick; that it was in some analogous manner she had flattered up March, Anson, and all the rest of the men that Mayne had spoken of. He supposed it was the first step in the process by which he was to be fooled, twisted round her finger, added to the list of victims who strewed her conquering path. He had a special fear of being fooled. For beneath a somewhat supercilious exterior, the dominant note of his character was timidity, distrust of his own merits; and he knew he was single-minded — one-idea'd almost — if he were to let himself go, to get to care very much for a woman, for such a girl as this girl, for instance, he would lose himself completely, be at her mercy absolutely. Fortunately, Mayne had let him know her character. He could feel nothing but dislike for her, — disgust, even. And yet he was conscious how pleasant it would be to believe in her innocence, in her candor. For she was so adorably pretty; her flower-like beauty grew upon him; her head, drooping a little on one side when she looked up, was so like a flower bent by its own weight. The texture of her cheeks, her lips, was delicious as the petals of a flower. He found he could recall with perfect accuracy every detail of her appearance; the manner in which the red hair grew round her temples; the way in which it was loosely and gracefully fastened up behind with just a single tortoise-shell pin. He recollected the suspicion of a dimple that shadowed itself in her cheek when she spoke, and deepened into a delicious reality every time she smiled. He remembered her throat: her hands, of a beautiful whiteness, with pink palms and pointed fingers. It was impossible to write. He speculated long on the ring she wore on her engaged finger. He mentioned this ring to Mayne the next time he saw him.

"Engaged? very much so, I should say. Has got a *fiancé* in every capital of Europe probably. But the ring-man is the *fiancé en titre*. He writes to her by every mail, and is tremendously in love with her. She shows me his letters. When she's had her fling, I suppose, she'll go back and marry him. That's what these little American girls do, I'm told; sow their wild oats here with us, and settle down into *bonnes ménagères* over yonder. Meanwhile, are you having any fun with her? Aha, she presses your hand? the 'gesegnete Mahlzeit' business after dinner is an excellent institution, isn't it? She'll tell you how much she loves you soon; that's the next move in the game."

But so far she had done neither of these things, for Campbell gave her no opportunities. He was guarded in the extreme, ungenial; avoiding her even at the cost of civility. Sometimes he was downright rude. That especially occurred when he felt himself inclined to yield to her advances. For she made him all sorts of silent advances, speaking with her eyes, her sad little mouth, her beseeching attitude. And then one evening she went further still. It occurred after dinner in the little green drawing-room. The rest of the company were gathered together in the big drawing-room beyond. The small room has deep embrasures to the windows. Each embrasure holds two old faded green velvet sofas in black oaken frames, and an oaken oblong table stands between them. Campbell had flung himself down on one of these sofas in the corner nearest the window. Miss Thayer, passing through the room, saw him, and sat down opposite. She leaned her elbows on the table, the laces of her sleeves falling away from her round white arms, and clasped her hands.

"Mr. Campbell, tell me what have I done? How have I vexed you? You have hardly spoken two words to me all day. You always try to avoid me." And when he began to utter evasive banalities, she stopped him with an imploring "Ah, don't! I love you. You know I love you. I love you so much I can't bear you to put me off with mere phrases."

Campbell admired the well-simulated passion

in her voice, remembered Mayne's prediction, and laughed aloud.

"Oh, you may laugh," she said, "but I am serious. I love you, I love you with my whole soul." She slipped round the end of the table, and came close beside him. His first impulse was to rise; then he resigned himself to stay. But it was not so much resignation that was required as self-mastery, cool-headedness. Her close proximity, her fragrance, those wonderful eyes raised so beseechingly to his, made his heart beat.

"Why are you so cold?" she said. "I love you so; can't you love me a little too?"

"My dear young lady," said Campbell, gently repelling her, "what do you take me for? A foolish boy like your friends Anson and March? What you are saying is monstrous, preposterous. Ten days ago you'd never even seen me."

"What has length of time to do with it?" she said. "I loved you at first sight."

"I wonder," he observed judicially, and again gently removed her hand from his, "to how many men you have not already said the same thing."

"I've never meant it before," she said quite earnestly, and nestled closer to him, and kissed the breast of his coat, and held her mouth up towards his. But he kept his chin resolutely high, and looked over her head.

"How many men have you not already kissed ever since you 've been here?"

"But there 've not been many here to kiss!" she exclaimed naïvely.

"Well, there was March; you kissed him?"

"No, I 'm quite sure I did n't."

"And young Anson; what about him? Ah, you don't answer! And then the other fellow — what 's his name — Prendergast — you 've kissed him?"

"But, after all, what is there in a kiss?" she cried ingenuously. "It means nothing, absolutely nothing. Why, one has to kiss all sorts of people one does n't care about."

Campbell remembered how Mayne had said she had probably known strange kisses since the age of ten; and a wave of anger with her, of righteous indignation, rose within him.

"To me," said he, "to all right-thinking people, a young girl's kisses are something pure, something sacred, not to be offered indiscriminately to every fellow she meets. Ah, you don't know what you have lost! You have seen a fruit that has been handled, that has lost its bloom?

THE PLEASURE-PILGRIM.

You have seen primroses, spring flowers, gathered and thrown away in the dust? And who enjoys the one, or picks up the others? And this is what you remind me of, — only you have deliberately, of your own perverse will, tarnished your beauty, and thrown away all the modesty, the reticence, the delicacy, which make a young girl so infinitely dear. You revolt me, you disgust me. I want nothing from you but to be let alone. Kindly take your hands away, and let me go."

He shook her roughly off and got up, then felt a moment's curiosity to see how she would take the repulse.

Miss Thayer never blushed; had never, he imagined, in her life done so. No faintest trace of color now stained the warm pallor of her rose-leaf skin; but her eyes filled up with tears. Two drops gathered on the under lashes, grew large, trembled an instant, and then rolled unchecked down her cheeks. Those tears somehow put him in the wrong, and he felt he had behaved brutally to her for the rest of the night.

He began to seek excuses for her: after all, she meant no harm; it was her upbringing, her *genre;* it was a *genre* he loathed; but perhaps he need not have spoken so harshly. He thought he would find a more friendly word for her next morning; and he loitered about the Mahlsaal, where the boarders come in to breakfast, as in an hotel, just when it suits them, till past eleven; but she did not come. Then, when he was almost tired of waiting, Miss Dodge put in an appearance, in a flannel wrapper, and her front hair twisted up in steel pins.

Campbell judged Miss Dodge with even more severity than he did Miss Thayer; there was nothing in this weird little creature's appearance to temper justice with mercy. It was with difficulty that he brought himself to inquire after her friend

"Lulie is sick this morning," she told him. "I've come down to order her some broth. She couldn't sleep any last night, because of your unkindness to her. She's vurry, vurry unhappy about it."

"Yes, I'm sorry for what I said. I had no right to speak so strongly, I suppose. But I spoke strongly because I feel strongly. However, there's no reason why my bad manners should make her unhappy."

"Oh, yes, there's vurry good reason," said

Miss Dodge. "She's vurry much in love with you."

Campbell looked at the speaker long and earnestly to try and read her mind; but the prominent blinking eyes, the cryptic physiognomy, told him nothing.

"Look here," he said brusquely, "what's your object in trying to fool me like this? I know all about your friend. Mayne has told me. She has cried 'Wolf' too often before to expect to be believed now."

"But, after all," argued Miss Dodge, blinking more than ever behind her glasses, "the wolf did really come at last, you know; did n't he? Lulie is really in love this time. We've all made mistakes in our lives, have n't we? But that's no reason for not being right at last. And Lulie has cried herself sick."

Campbell was a little shaken. He went and repeated the conversation to Mayne, who laughed derisively.

"Capital, capital!" he cried; "excellently contrived. It quite supports my latest theory about our young friend. She's an actress, a born comédienne. She acts always, and to every one: to you, to me, to the Ritterhausens, to the Dodge girl — even to herself when she is quite alone. And she has a great respect for her art; she'll carry out her rôle, *coûte que coûte*, to the bitter end. She chooses to pose as in love with you; you don't respond; the part now requires that she should sicken and pine. Consequently she takes to her bed, and sends her confidante to tell you so. Oh, it's colossal, it's *famos*."

IV.

"IF you can't really love me," said Lulie Thayer, — "and I know I've been a bad girl and don't deserve that you should, — at least, will you allow me to go on loving you?"

She walked by Campbell's side, through the solitary uncared-for park of Schloss Altenau. It was three weeks later in the year, and the spring feeling in the air stirred the blood. All round were signs and tokens of spring: in the busy gayety of bird and insect life; in the purple flower-tufts which thickened the boughs of the ash-trees; in the young green things pushing up pointed heads from amidst last season's dead leaves and grasses. The snow-wreaths, that had for so long decorated the distant hills, were shrinking perceptibly away beneath the strong March sunshine.

There was every invitation to spend one's time out of doors, and Campbell passed long mornings in the park, or wandering through the woods and the surrounding villages. Miss Thayer often accompanied him. He never invited her to do so, but when she offered him her company, he could not, or at least did not, refuse it.

"May I love you? Say," she entreated.

"'Wenn ich Dich liebe, was geht's Dich an?'" he quoted lightly. "Oh, no, it's nothing to me, of course. Only don't expect me to believe you, — that's all."

This disbelief of his was the recurring decimal of their conversation. No matter on what subject they began, they always ended thus. And the more sceptical he showed himself, the more eager she became. She exhausted herself in endeavors to convince him.

They had reached the corner in the park where the road to the Castle turns off at right angles from the road to Dürrendorf. The ground rises gently on the park-side to within three feet of the top of the boundary wall, although on the other side there is a drop of at least twenty feet. The broad wall-top makes a convenient seat. Campbell and the girl sat down on it; at his last words she wrung her hands together in her lap.

"But how can you disbelieve me?" she cried, "when I tell you I love you, I adore you? When I swear it to you? And can't you see for yourself? Why, every one at the Castle sees it."

"Yes, you afford the Castle a good deal of unnecessary amusement. And that shows you don't understand what love really is. Real love is full of delicacy, of reticences, and would feel itself profaned if it became the jest of the servants' hall."

"It's not so much my love for you, as your rejection of it, which has made me talked about."

"Isn't it rather on account of the favors you've lavished on all my predecessors?"

She sprang to her feet, and walked up and down in agitation.

"But after all, surely, mistakes of that sort are not to be counted against us? I did really think I was in love with Mr. March. Willie Anson doesn't count. He's an American too, and he understands things. Besides, he is only a boy. And how could I know I should love you before I had met you? And how can I help loving you now I have? You're so different from other men. You're good, you're honorable, you treat women with respect. Oh, I do love you so, I do love you! Ask Nannie if I don't."

The way in which Campbell shrugged his shoulders clearly expressed the amount of reliance he would place on any testimony from Miss Dodge. He could not forget her "Why don't you make love to Lulie?" addressed to a married man. Such a want of principle argued an equal want of truth.

Lulie seemed on the brink of weeping.

"I wish I were dead," she struggled to say; "life's impossible if you won't believe me. I don't ask you any longer to love me. I know I've been a bad girl, and I don't deserve that you should; but if you won't believe that I love you I don't want to live any longer."

Campbell confessed to himself that she acted admirably, but that the damnable iteration of the one idea became monotonous. He sought a change of subject. "Look there," he said, "close by the wall, what's that jolly little blue flower? It's the first I've seen this year."

He showed her where, at the base of the wall, a solitary blossom rose above a creeping stem and glossy dark green leaves.

Lulie, all smiles again, picked it with child-like pleasure. "Oh, if that's the first you've seen," she cried, "you can take a wish. Only you mustn't speak until some one asks you a question.

She began to fasten it in his coat. "It's just as blue as your eyes," she said. "You have such blue and boyish eyes, you know. Stop, stop, that's not a question," and, seeing that he was about to speak, she laid her finger across his mouth. "You'll spoil the charm."

She stepped back, folded her arms, and seemed to dedicate herself to eternal silence; then relenting suddenly,—

"Do you believe me?" she entreated.

"What's become of your ring?" Campbell answered beside the mark. He had noticed its absence from her finger while she had been fixing in the flower.

"Oh, my engagement's broken."

Campbell asked how the *fiancé* would like that.

"Oh, he won't mind. He knows I only got engaged because he worried so. And it was always understood between us that I was to be free if I ever met any one I liked better."

Campbell asked her what sort of fellow this accommodating *fiancé* was.

"Oh, he's all right. And he's very good too. But he's not a bit clever, and don't let us talk about him. He makes me tired."

"But you're wrong," Campbell told her, "to throw away a good, a sincere affection. If you really want to reform and turn over a new leaf, as you are always telling me you do, I should advise you to go home and marry him."

"What, when I'm in love with you?" she cried reproachfully. "Would that be right?"

"It's going to rain," said Campbell. "Did n't you feel a drop just then? And it's getting near lunch-time. Shall we go in?"

Their shortest way led through the little cemetery in which the departed Ritterhausens lay at peace in the shadow of their sometime home.

"When I die the Baron has promised I shall be buried here," said Lulie pensively; "just here, next to his first wife. Don't you think it would be lovely to be buried in a beautiful, peaceful baronial graveyard, instead of in some horrid crowded city cemetery?"

Mayne met them as they entered the hall. He noticed the flower in his friend's coat. "Ah, my dear chap, been treading the — periwinkle path of dalliance, I see? How many desirable young men have I not witnessed led down the same broad way by the same seductive lady! Always the same thing; nothing changes but the flower according to the season."

When Campbell reached his room he took the poor periwinkle out of his coat, and threw it away into the stove.

And yet, had it not been for Mayne, Miss Thayer might have triumphed after all; might have convinced Campbell of her passion, or have added another victim to her long list. But Mayne had set himself as determinedly to spoil her game as she was bent on winning it. He had always the cynical word, the apt reminiscence ready, whenever he saw signs on Campbell's part of surrender. He was very fond of Campbell. He did not wish him to fall a prey to the wiles of this little American siren. He had watched her conduct in the past with a dozen different men; he genuinely believed she was only acting in the present.

Campbell, for his part, began to experience

an ever-increasing exasperation in the girl's presence. Yet he did not avoid it; he could not well avoid it, she followed him about so persistently; but his speech would overflow with bitterness towards her. He would say the cruellest things; then, remembering them when alone, be ashamed of his brutalities. But nothing he said ever altered her sweetness of temper or weakened the tenacity of her purpose. His rebuffs made her beautiful eyes run over with tears, but the harshest of them never elicited the least sign of resentment. There would have been something touching as well as comic in this dog-like humility, which accepted everything as welcome at his hands, had he not been imbued with Mayne's conviction that it was all an admirable piece of acting. Or when for a moment he forgot the histrionic theory, then invariably there would come a chance word in her conversation which would fill him with cold rage. They would be talking of books, travels, sport, what not, and she would drop a reference to this man or to that. So-and-so had taken her to Bullier's, she had learned skating with this other; Duroy, the *prix de Rome* man, had painted her as Hebe; Franz Weber had tried to teach her German by means of Heine's poems. And he got glimpses of long vistas of amourettes played in every State in America, in every country of Europe, since the very beginning, when, as a mere child, elderly men, friends of her father's, had held her on their knee and fed her on sweetmeats and kisses. It was sickening to think of, it was pitiable. So much youth and beauty tarnished; the possibility for so much good thrown away. For if one could only blot out her record, forget it, accept her for what she chose to appear, a more endearing companion no man could desire.

V.

It was a wet afternoon, the rain had set in at midday with a gray determination which gave no hopes of clearing. Nevertheless, Mayne had accompanied his wife and the Baroness into Hamelin. "To take up a servant's character, and expostulate with a recalcitrant dressmaker," he explained to Campbell, and wondered what women would do to fill up their days were it not for the perennial crimes of dressmakers and domestic servants. He himself was going to look in at the English Club; wouldn't Campbell come too? There was a fourth seat in the carriage. But Campbell was in no social mood; he felt his temper going all to pieces; a quarter of an hour of Mrs. Mayne's society would have brought on an explosion. He thought he must be alone; and yet when he had read for half an hour in his room he wondered vaguely what Lulie was doing; he had not seen her since luncheon. She always gave him her society when he could very well dispense with it, but on a wet day like this, when a little conversation would be tolerable, of course she stayed away. Then there came down the long Rittersaal the tapping of high heels, and a well-known knock at his door. He went over and opened it; Miss Thayer, in the plush and lace tea-gown, fronted him serenely.

"Am I disturbing you?" she asked; and his mood was so capricious that, now she was standing there on his threshold, he thought he was annoyed at it. "It's so dull," she said, persuasively. "Nannie's got a sick headache, and I daren't go downstairs, or the Baron will annex me to play Halma. He always wants to play Halma on wet days."

"And what do you want to do?" said Campbell, leaning against the doorpost, and letting his eyes rest on the strange piquant face in its setting of red hair.

"To be with you, of course."

"Well," said he, coming out and closing the door, "I'm at your service. What next?"

They strolled together through the room, and listened to the falling rain. The Rittersaal occupies all the space on the first floor that the hall and four drawing-rooms do below. Wooden pillars support the ceiling, dividing the apartment lengthwise into a nave and two aisles. Down the middle are long tables used for ceremonial banquets. Six windows look into the courtyard, and six out over the open country. The centre pane of each window is emblazoned with a Ritterhausen shield. Between the windows hang family portraits, and the sills are broad and low, and cushioned in faded velvet.

"How it rains!" said Lulie, stopping before one of the south windows; "why, you can't see anything for the rain, and there's no sound at all but the rain either. I like it. It makes me feel as though we had the whole world to ourselves."

Then, "Say, what would you like to do?" she asked him. "Shall I fetch over my pistols, and we'll practise with them? You've no notion how well I can shoot. We couldn't hurt anything here, could we?"

Campbell thought they might practise there without inconvenience, and Lulie, bundling up the duchess tea-gown over one arm, danced off in very unduchess-like fashion to fetch the case.

It was a charming little box of cedar-wood and mother-o'-pearl, lined with violet velvet; and two tiny revolvers lay inside, hardly more than six inches long, with silver engraved handles.

"I won them in a bet," she observed complacently, "with the Hon. Billie Thornton. He's an Englishman, you know, the son of Lord Thornton. I knew him in Washington two years ago last fall. He bet I couldn't hit a three-cent piece at twenty yards, and I did. Aren't they perfectly sweet? Now, can't you contrive a target?"

Campbell went back to his room, drew out a rough diagram, and pasted it down on to a piece of cardboard. Then this was fixed up by means of a penknife driven into the wood of one of the pillars, and Campbell, with his walking-stick laid down six successive times, measured off the distance required, and set a chalk mark across the floor. Lulie took the first shot. She held the little weapon up at arm's length above her head, the first finger stretched out along the barrel; then, dropping her hand sharply so that the finger pointed straight at the butt, she pulled the trigger with the third. There was the sharp report, the tiny smoke film; and when Campbell went up to examine results, he found she had only missed the very centre by a quarter of an inch.

Lulie was exultant. "I don't seem to have got out of practice any," she remarked. "I'm so glad, for I used to be a very good shot. It was Hiram P. Ladd who taught me. He's the crack shot of Montana. What! you don't know Hiram P.? Why, I should have supposed every one must have heard of him. He had the next ranche to my Uncle Samuel's, where I used to go summers, and he made me do an hour's pistol practice every morning after bathing. It was he who taught me swimming too — in the river."

"Damnation," said Campbell under his breath, then shot in his turn, and shot wide. Lulie made another bull's-eye, and after that a white. She urged Campbell to continue, which he sullenly did, and again missed.

"You see I don't come up to your Hiram P. Ladd," he remarked savagely, and put the pistol down, and walked over to the window. He stood with one foot on the cushioned seat, staring out at the rain, and pulling moodily at his moustache.

Lulie followed him, nestled up to him, lifted the hand that hung passive by his side, put it round her waist and held it there. Campbell, lost in thought, let it remain so for a second; then remembered how she had doubtless done this very same thing with other men in this very room. All her apparently spontaneous movements, he told himself, were but the oft-used pieces in the game she played so skilfully.

"Let go," he said, and flung himself down on the window-seat, looking up at her with darkening eyes.

She, sitting meekly in the other corner, folded her offending hands in her lap.

"Do you know your eyes are not a bit nice when you're cross?" she said; "they seem to become quite black."

He maintained a discouraging silence.

She looked over at him meditatively.

"I never cared a bit for Hiram P., if that's what you mean," she remarked presently.

"Do you suppose I care a button if you did?"

"Then why did you leave off shooting, and why won't you talk to me?"

He vouchsafed no reply.

Lulie spent some moments immersed in thought. Then she sighed deeply, and recommenced on a note of pensive regret: —

"Ah, if I'd only met you sooner in life, I should be a very different girl."

The freshness which her quaint, drawling enunciation lent to this time-dishonored formula made Campbell smile, till, remembering all its implications, his forehead set in frowns again.

Lulie continued her discourse. "You see," said she, "I never had any one to teach me what was right. My mother died when I was quite a child, and my father has always let me do exactly as I pleased, so long as I didn't bother him. Then I've never had a home, but have always lived around in hotels and places: all winter in New York or Washington, and summers out at Longbranch or Saratoga. It's true we own a house in Detroit, on Lafayette

Avenue, that we reckon as home, but we don't ever go there. It's a bad sort of life for a girl, isn't it?" she pleaded.

"Horrible," he said mechanically. His mind was at work. The loose threads of his angers, his irritations, his desires, were knitting themselves together, weaving themselves into something overmastering and definite.

The young girl meanwhile was moving up towards him along the seat, for the effect which his sharpest rebuke produced on her never lasted more than four minutes. She now again possessed herself of his hand, and, holding it between her own, began to caress it in childlike fashion, pulling the fingers apart and closing them again, spreading it palm downwards on her lap, and laying her own little hand over it, to exemplify the differences between them. He let her be; he seemed unconscious of her proceedings.

"And then," she continued, "I've always known a lot of young fellows who've liked to take me round; and no one ever objected to my going with them, and so I went. And I enjoyed it, and there wasn't any harm in it, just kissing, and making believe, and nonsense. But I never really cared for one of them. I can see that now, when I compare them with you, — when I compare what I felt for them with what I feel for you. Oh, I do love you so much," she murmured; "don't you believe me?" She lifted his hand to her lips and covered it with kisses.

He pulled it roughly from her. "I wish you'd give over such fool's play," he told her, got up, walked to the table, came back again, stood looking at her with sombre eyes and dilating pupils.

"But I do love you," she repeated, rising and advancing towards him.

"For God's sake, drop that damned rot," he cried out with sudden fury. "It wearies me, do you hear? it sickens me. Love, love, my God, what do you know about it? Why, if you really loved me, really loved any man, — if you had any conception of what the passion of love is, how beautiful, how fine, how sacred, — the mere idea that you could not come to your lover fresh, pure, untouched, as a young girl should, that you had been handled, fondled, and God knows what besides, by this man and the other, — would fill you with such horror for yourself, with such supreme disgust, you would feel yourself so unworthy, so polluted . . .

that . . . that . . . by God! you would take up that pistol there, and blow your brains out!"

Lulie seemed to find the idea quite entertaining. She picked the pistol up from where it lay in the window, examined it critically, with her pretty head drooping on one side, and then sent one of her long, red-brown caressing glances up towards him.

"And suppose I were to," she asked lightly, "would you believe me then?"

"Oh, . . . well . . . then, perhaps! If you showed sufficient decency to kill yourself, perhaps I might," said he, with ironical laughter. His ebullition had relieved him; his nerves were calmed again. "But nothing short of that would ever make me."

With her little tragic air, which seemed to him so like a smile disguised, she raised the weapon to the bosom of her gown. There came a sudden, sharp crack, a tiny smoke-film. She stood an instant swaying slightly, smiling certainly, distinctly outlined against the background of rain-washed window, of gray falling rain, the top of her head cutting in two the Ritterhausen escutcheon. Then all at once there was nothing at all between him and the window; he saw the coat-of-arms entire; but a motionless, inert heap of plush and lace, and fallen wine-red hair, lay at his feet upon the floor.

"Child, child, what have you done?" he cried with anguish, and, kneeling beside her, lifted her up, and looked into her face.

When from a distance of time and place Campbell was at last able to look back with some degree of calmness on the catastrophe, the element in it which stung him most keenly was this: he could never convince himself that Lulie had really loved him after all. And the only two persons who had known them both and the circumstances of the case sufficiently well to have resolved his doubts one way or the other, held diametrically opposite views.

"Well, listen, then, and I'll tell you how it was," Miss Nannie Dodge had said to him impressively, the day before he left Schloss Altenau forever. "Lulie was tremendously, terribly in love with you. And when she found that you wouldn't care about her, she didn't want to live any more. As to the way in which it happened, you don't need to reproach yourself for that. She'd have done it, anyhow; if not then, why, later. But it's all the rest of your conduct to her that was so mean, your cold, cruel, complacent British unresponsiveness. I guess you'll never find another woman to love you as Lulie did. She was just the darlingest, the sweetest, the most loving girl in the world."

Mayne, on the other hand, summed it up in this way: "Of course, old chap, it's horrible to think of; horrible, horrible, horrible! I can't tell you how badly I feel about it. For she was a gorgeously beautiful creature. That red hair of hers — Good Lord! You won't come across such hair as that again in a lifetime. But, believe me, she was only fooling with you. Once she had you in her hunting-noose, once her buccaneering instincts satisfied, and she'd have chucked you as she did all the rest. As to her death, I've got three theories, — no, two, — for the first being that she compassed it in a moment of genuine emotion, we may dismiss, I think, as quite untenable. The second is, that it arose from pure misadventure. You had both been shooting, hadn't you? Well, she took up the pistol and pulled the trigger from mere mischief, to frighten you, and quite forgetting one barrel was still loaded. And the third is, it was just her histrionic sense of the fitness of things. The rôle she had played so long and so well now demanded a sensational finale in the centre of the stage. And it's the third theory I give the preference to. She was the most consummate little actress I ever met."

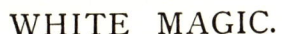

WHITE MAGIC.

I SPENT one evening last summer with my friend Mauger, *pharmacien* in the little town of Jacques-le-Port. He pronounces his name Major, by the by, it being a quaint custom of the Islands to write proper names one way and speak them another, thus serving to bolster up that old, old story of the German savant's account of the difficulties of the English language, — "where you spell a man's name Verulam," says he reproachfully, "and pronounce it Bacon."

Mauger and I sat in the pleasant wood-panelled parlor behind the shop, from whence all sorts of aromatic odors found their way in through the closed door to mingle with the fragrance of figs, Ceylon tea, and hot *gôches-à-beurre*, constituting the excellent meal spread before us. The large old-fashioned windows were wide open, and I looked straight out upon the harbor, filled with holiday yachts, and the wonderful azure sea.

Over against the other islands, opposite, a gleam of white streaked the water, white clouds hung motionless in the blue sky, and a tiny boat with white sails passed out round Falla Point. A white butterfly entered the room to flicker in gay uncertain curves above the cloth, and a warm reflected light played over the slender rat-tailed forks and spoons, and raised by a tone or two the color of Mauger's tanned face and yellow beard. For, in spite of a sedentary profession, his preferences lie with an out-of-door life, and he takes an afternoon off whenever practicable, as he had done that day, to follow his favorite pursuit over the golf-links at Les Landes.

While he had been deep in the mysteries of teeing and putting, with no subtler problem to be solved than the judicious selection of mashie and cleek, I had explored some of the curious cromlechs or *pouquelayes* scattered over this part of the island, and my thoughts and speech harked back irresistibly to the strange old religions and usages of the past.

"Science is all very well in its way," said I; "and of course it's an inestimable advantage to inhabit this so-called nineteenth century; but the mediæval want of science was far more picturesque. The once universal belief in charms and portents, in wandering saints and fighting fairies, must have lent an interest to life which these prosaic days sadly lack. Madelon then would steal from her bed on moonlight nights in May, and slip across the dewy grass with naked feet, to seek the reflection of her future husband's face in the first running stream she passed; now, Miss Mary Jones puts on her bonnet and steps round the corner, on no more romantic errand than the investment of her month's wages in the savings bank at two and a half per cent."

Mauger laughed. "I wish she did anything half so prudent! That has not been my experience of the Mary Joneses."

"Well, anyhow," I insisted, "the Board School has rationalized them. It has pulled up the innate poetry of their nature to replace it by decimal fractions."

To which Mauger answered, "Rot!" and offered me his cigarette-case. After the first few silent whiffs, he went on as follows: "The innate poetry of Woman! Confess now, there is no more unpoetic creature under the sun.

Offer her the sublimest poetry ever written and the 'Daily Telegraph's' latest article on fashions, or a good sound murder or reliable divorce, and there's no betting on her choice, for it's a dead certainty. Many men have a love of poetry, but I'm inclined to think that a hundred women out of ninety-nine positively dislike it."

Which struck me as true. "We'll drop the poetry, then," I answered; "but my point remains, that if the girl of to-day has no superstitions, the girl of to-morrow will have no beliefs. Teach her to sit down thirteen to table, to spill the salt, and walk under a ladder with equanimity, and you open the door for Spencer and Huxley, and, — and all the rest of it," said I, coming to an impotent conclusion.

"Oh, if superstition were the salvation of woman, — but you are thinking of young ladies in London, I suppose? Here, in the Islands, I can show you as much superstition as you please. I'm not sure that the country-people in their heart of hearts don't still worship the old gods of the *pouquelayes*. You would not, of course, find any one to own up to it, or to betray the least glimmer of an idea as to your meaning, were you to question him, for ours is a shrewd folk, wearing their orthodoxy bravely; but possibly the old beliefs are cherished with the more ardor for not being openly avowed. Now you like bits of actuality. I'll give you one, and a proof, too, that the modern maiden is still separated by many a fathom of salt seawater from these fortunate isles.

"Some time ago, on a market morning, a girl came into the shop, and asked for some blood from a dragon. 'Some what?' said I, not catching her words. 'Well, just a little blood from a dragon,' she answered very tremulously, and blushing. She meant, of course, 'dragon's blood,' a resinous powder formerly much used in medicine, though out of fashion now.

"She was a pretty young creature, with pink cheeks and dark eyes, and a forlorn expression of countenance which did n't seem at all to fit in with her blooming health. Not from the town, or I should have known her face; evidently come from one of the country parishes to sell her butter and eggs. I was interested to discover what she wanted the 'dragon's blood' for, and after a certain amount of hesitation she told me. 'They do say it's good, sir, if anything should have happened betwixt you an' your young man.' 'Then you have a young man?' said I. 'Yes, sir.' 'And you've fallen out with him?' 'Yes, sir.' And tears rose to her eyes at the admission, while her mouth rounded with awe at my amazing perspicacity. 'And you mean to send him some dragon's blood as a love potion?' 'No, sir; you've got to mix it with water you've fetched from the Three Sisters' Well, and drink it yourself in nine sips on nine nights running, and get into bed without once looking in the glass; and then if you've done everything properly, and haven't made any mistake, he'll come back to you, an' love you twice as much as before.' 'And la Mère Todevinn (Tostevin) gave you that precious recipe, and made you cross her hand with silver into the bargain?' said I severely; on which the tears began to flow outright. .

"You know," said Mauger, breaking off his narration, "the old lady who lives in the curious stone house at the corner of the market-place? A reputed witch who learned both black and white magic from her mother, who was a daughter of Hélier Mouton, the famous sorcerer of Cakeuro. I could tell you some funny stories relating to la Mère Todevinn, who numbers more clients among the officers and fine ladies here than in any other class; and very curious, too, is the history of that stone house, with the Brancourt arms still sculptured on the side. You can see them, if you turn down by the Water-gate. This old sinister-looking building, or rather portion of a building, for more modern houses have been built over the greater portion of the site, and now press upon it from either hand, once belonged to one of the finest mansions in the Islands, but through a curse and a crime has been brought down to its present condition; while the Brancourt family has long since been utterly extinct. But all this is n't the story of Elsie Mahy, which turned out to be the name of my little customer.

"The Mahys are of the Vauvert parish, and Pierre Jean, the father of this girl, began life as a day laborer, took to tomato-growing on borrowed capital, and now owns a dozen glasshouses of his own. Mrs. Mahy does some dairy-farming on a minute scale, the profits of which she and Miss Elsie share as pin-money. The young man who is courting Elsie is a son of Toumes the builder. He probably had something to do with the putting up of Mahy's greenhouses, but anyhow, he has been constantly over at Vauvert during the last six months, superintending the alterations at de Câterelle's place.

"Toumes, it would seem, is a devoted but imperious lover, and the Persian and Median laws are as butter compared with the inflexibility of his decisions. The little rift within the lute, which has lately turned all the music to discord, occurred last Monday week, — bank-holiday, as you may remember. The Sunday-school to which Elsie belongs — and it's a strange anomaly, isn't it, that a girl going to Sunday-school should still have a rooted belief in white magic? — the school was to go for an outing to Prawn Bay, and Toumes had arranged to join his sweetheart at the starting-point. But he had made her promise that if by any chance he should be delayed, she would not go with the others, but would wait until he came to fetch her.

"Of course, it so happened that he *was* detained, and, equally of course, Elsie, like a true woman, went off without him. She did all she knew to make me believe she went quite against her own wishes, that her companions forced her to go. The beautifully yielding nature of a woman never comes out so conspicuously as when she is being coerced into following her own secret desires. Anyhow, Toumes, arriving some time later, found her gone. He followed on, and under ordinary circumstances, I suppose, a sharp reprimand would have been considered sufficient. Unfortunately, the young man arrived on the scene to find his truant love deep in the frolics of kiss-in-the-ring. After tea in the Câterelle Arms, the whole party had adjourned to a neighboring meadow, and were thus whiling away the time to the exhilarating strains of a French horn and a concertina. Elsie was led into the centre of the ring by various country bumpkins, and kissed beneath the eyes of heaven, of her neighbors, and of her embittered swain.

"You may have been amongst us long enough to know that the Toumes family are of a higher social grade than the Mahys, and I suppose the Misses Toumes never in their lives stooped to anything so ungenteel as public kiss-in-the-ring. It was not surprising, therefore, to hear that after this incident 'me an' my young man had words,' as Elsie put it.

"Note," said Mauger, "the descriptive truth of this expression 'having words.' Among the unlettered, lovers only do have words when vexed. At other times they will sit holding hands throughout a long summer's afternoon, and not exchange two remarks an hour. Love seals their tongue; anger alone unlooses it, and naturally, when unloosened, it runs on, from sheer want of practice, a great deal faster and further than they desire.

"So, life being thorny and youth being vain, they parted late that same evening, with the understanding that they would meet no more; and to be wroth with one we love worked its usual harrowing effects. Toumes took to billiards and brandy, Elsie to tears and invocations of Beelzebub; then came Mère Todevinn's recipe, my own more powerful potion, and now once more all is silence and balmy peace."

"Do you mean to tell me you sold the child a charm, and didn't enlighten her as to its futility?"

"I sold her some bicarbonate of soda worth a couple of *doubles*, and charged her five shillings for it into the bargain," said Mauger, unblushingly. "A wrinkle I learned from once

WHITE MAGIC. 231

overhearing an old lady I had treated for nothing expatiating to a crony, 'Eh, but, my good, my good! dat Mr. Major, I don't t'ink much of him. He give away his add-vice an' his meddecines for nuddin'. Dey not wurt nuddin' neider for sure.' So I made Elsie hand me over five British shillings, and I gave her the powder, and told her to drink it with her meals. But I threw in another prescription, which, if less important, must nevertheless be punctiliously carried out, if the charm was to have any effect. 'The very next time,' I told her, 'that you meet your young man in the street, walk straight up to him without looking to the right or to the left, and hold out your hand, saying these words: "Please, I so want to be friends again!" Then if you've been a good girl, have taken the powder regularly, and not forgotten one of my directions, you'll find that all will come right.'

"Now, little as you may credit it," said Mauger, smiling, "the charm worked, for all that we live in the so-called nineteenth century. Elsie came into the shop only yesterday to tell me the results, and to thank me very prettily. 'I shall always come to you now, sir,' she was good enough to say, 'I mean, if anything was to go wrong again. You know a great deal more than Mère Todevinn, I'm sure.' 'Yes, I'm a famous sorcerer,' said I, 'but you had better not speak about the powder. You are wise enough to see that it was just your own conduct in meeting your young man rather more than halfway, that did the trick — eh?' She looked at me with eyes brimming over with wisdom. 'You need n't be afraid, sir, I'll not speak of it. Mère Todevinn always made me promise to keep silence too. But of course I know it was the powder that worked the charm.'

"And to that belief the dear creature will stick to the last day of her life. Women are wonderful enigmas. Explain to them that tight-lacing displaces all the internal organs, and show them diagrams to illustrate your point, they smile sweetly, say, 'Oh, how funny!' and go out to buy their new stays half an inch smaller than their old ones. But tell them they must never pass a pin in the street for luck's sake, if it lies with its point towards them, and they will sedulously look for and pick up every such confounded pin they see. Talk to a woman of the marvels of science, and she turns a deaf ear, or refuses point-blank to believe you; yet she is absolutely all ear for any old wife's tale, drinks it greedily in, and never loses hold of it for the rest of her days."

"But does she?" said I; "that's the point in dispute; and though your story shows there's still a commendable amount of superstition in the Islands, I'm afraid if you were to come to London, you would not find sufficient to cover a threepenny-piece."

"Woman is woman all the world over," said Mauger, sententiously, "no matter what mental garb happens to be in fashion at the time. *Grattez la femme, et vous trouvez la folle.* For see here: if I had said to Mademoiselle Elsie, 'Well, you were in the wrong; it's your place to take the first step towards reconciliation,' she would have laughed in my face, or flung out of the shop in a rage. But because I sold her a little humbugging powder under the guise of a charm, she submitted herself with the docility of a pet lambkin. No; one need never hope to prevail through wisdom with a woman, and if I could have realized that ten years ago, it would have been better for me."

He fell silent, thinking of his past, which to me, who knew it, seemed almost an excuse for his cynicism. I sought a change of idea. The splendor of the pageant outside supplied me with one.

The sun had set; and all the eastern world of sky and water, stretching before us, was steeped in the glories of the after-glow. The ripples seemed painted in dabs of ruddy gold upon a surface of polished blue-gray steel. Over the islands opposite hung a far-reaching golden cloud, with faint-drawn, up-curled edges, as though thinned out upon the sky by some monster brush; and while I watched it, this cloud changed from gold to rose-color, and instantly the steel mirror of the sea glowed rosy too, and was streaked and shaded with a wonderful rosy-brown. As the color grew momentarily more intense in the sky above, so did the sea appear to pulse to a more vivid copperish-rose, until at last it was like nothing so much as a sea of flowing fire. And the cloud flamed fiery too, yet all the while its upcurled edges rested in exquisite contrast upon a background of most cool cerulean blue.

The little sailing-boat, which I had noticed an hour previously, reappeared from behind the Point. The sail was lowered as it entered the harbor, and the boatman took to his oars. I watched it creep over the glittering water until it vanished beneath the window-sill. I got up and went over to the window to hold it still in sight. It was sculled by a young man in rosy shirt-sleeves, and opposite to him, in the stern, sat a girl in a rosy gown.

So long as I had observed them, not one word had either spoken. In silence they had crossed the harbor, in silence the sculler had brought his craft alongside the landing-stage, and secured her to a ring in the stones. Still silent, he helped his companion to step out upon the quay.

"Here," said I to Mauger, "is a couple confirming your 'silent' theory with a vengeance. We must suppose that much love has rendered them absolutely dumb."

He came and leaned from the window too.

"It's not *a* couple, but *the* couple," said he; "and after all, in spite of cheap jesting, there are some things more eloquent than speech." For at this instant, finding themselves alone upon the jetty, the young man had taken the girl into his arms, and she had lifted a frank responsive mouth to return his kiss.

Five minutes later the sea had faded into dull grays and sober browns, starved white clouds moved dispiritedly over a vacant sky, and by cricking the back of my neck I was able to follow Toumes' black coat and the white frock of Miss Elsie until they reached Poidevin's wine-vaults, and, turning up the Water-gate, were lost to view.

THE EXPIATION OF DAVID SCOTT.

THE EXPIATION OF DAVID SCOTT.

I.

Mr. David Scott sat one morning immersed in business. To and fro from his desk, clerks passed continually to the outer room, whence, during the momentary opening of the swing-doors, the rapid driving of pens on paper was distinctly audible.

Towards mid-day the pressure of work in outer and inner office slackened; the handsome presentation clock chiming a quarter to one reminded Scott to take the prescribed tonic standing there on the mantelpiece before him. But it was rather to please his daughter Catherine that he poured it out and drank it, than because he had any belief in it himself, as it had been to please her that he had recently consulted a famous city physician about his health. The great man had rounded many sonorous phrases, which to a less shrewd patient than Scott would have proved, for a time, amply satisfying. But Scott understood he was in a precarious condition; he said to himself his days were numbered, and he was grateful to Providence for timely warning before the end.

The medicine was bitter; he turned to get a biscuit to take away the taste. Then he changed his mind, putting up with the bitterness instead. He frequently practised unobserved mortifications of this sort, with the idea of atonement; yet his unblemished reputation and religious life were the edification of all who knew him. It is, however, only the really pious who suffer from conscience.

A clerk entered with a card and a letter. On the card was printed "Mr. James O'Brien," and written beneath, in pencil, "from New York;" the letter was in the well-known hand of one of Scott's correspondents in that city, and contained a friendly request that Scott would do everything in his power for the gentleman presenting it.

Scott gave orders for Mr. O'Brien's admission. During the few seconds that elapsed before the entry of the visitor, he sat with the open letter under his hand, and a presentiment of trouble in his heart. He was sensibly

THE EXPIATION OF DAVID SCOTT.

relieved when a total stranger to him walked into the room.

"Mr. David Scott?" asked the visitor promptly, with a slight American accent.

Scott assented with a bow, and indicated a seat.

The full light from the window fell upon the stranger's face; but Scott, having shifted his chair, sat in shadow. One naturally takes such an advantage as this on one's own premises. Scott saw a man in the prime of life, with a tanned skin, piercing eyes, and a gloomy expression; he had short iron-gray hair and a dark moustache that completely concealed his mouth. His clothes were neither new nor good, but he wore them well; and, fixing his interlocutor with his keen glance, he seemed capable of paralyzing you from observing that his boots were broken and his coat had lost its nap.

Scott at first took him to be a military man; but on noting the wary and dogged determination of his face, — which only comes from confronting the varied and undisciplined ills of civil life, — he concluded O'Brien had seen service in both careers.

He took up the card again, and looked at it meditatively.

"In what way can I be of any assistance?" he asked.

"Perhaps my name is not unknown to you?" returned the visitor.

Scott hesitated. In truth, the name was connected with a melancholy passage in his history, and every time he came across it since, — and he was constantly coming across it, — it acted as a key to unlock the secret troubles of the past.

"I have met a good many O'Briens in the course of my life," said he, collecting his thoughts; and added, with a smile, "the king, your ancestor, was a man of large family."

O'Brien smiled too, but without geniality.

"To be sure; there are a good many of us about, and we all descend from kings. But not to detain you unnecessarily, private affairs of importance have brought me to England, and pending their settlement, it is essential I should obtain some employment, having no private means. I was fortunate enough to make the acquaintance of Mr. Rezin E. Van Hannen of N' York, and he kindly gave me the letter of introduction to you."

"I should, of course, be very glad to oblige any of the Van Hannens," said Scott, slowly;

"they have put a good deal of business in my way."

But he was wondering to himself how he could be expected to find work for a man of O'Brien's age, and how it was that, despite the stranger's capable and even impressive appearance, he should thus be reduced to begging a place in the city, like the most incompetent of city clerks. Yet he was interested in him too, — the name in itself was sufficient to rivet his interest, — and then there was a tone of voice, a trick of manner, Scott found attractive. He put a few questions as to the kind of employment desired.

"I'm not particular," answered O'Brien. "I would do anything at all. Indeed, at one time or another I've done everything already, from gum-digging in New Zealand to log-rolling in Manitoba. I've worked with my hands, and I've worked with my head, and ill-luck has pursued me all the world round." He laughed rather bitterly. "I've heard people doubt whether there's a Power of Good to direct man's actions, but there seems no doubt at all that there's a very active Principle of Evil."

"What appears to us evil," said Scott, "is

often good in disguise; and it not seldom happens that those lives outwardly the most prosperous and enviable are in reality the most to be pitied."

Perhaps he was thinking of the insidious disease which had laid its hold on him; the pain in his side, one of its most troublesome symptoms, was keen just then. But O'Brien answered from his own point of view.

"People who have enjoyed every material prosperity are fond of indulging in imaginary troubles. To have knocked about two hemispheres as I have done would soon cure them; and to have known the want of a crust of bread or glass of water, makes a man not only grateful, but cheerful under moderate good fortune."

"Yes, indeed," said Scott; "those are hardships one rarely encounters. I was referring to other trials, as real perhaps to some minds, though less tangible. But you must have seen strange times. Van Hannen tells me here you have had some curious experiences?"

"I have gone through as many unpleasant adventures as are to be found in a dime novel, and now, after twenty years' wandering, find myself home again at last."

"Twenty years!" repeated Scott, struck

THE EXPIATION OF DAVID SCOTT. 245

by the coincidence in date with memories of his own. "After twenty years you must find many changes, not only in London itself, — though that is altering very rapidly, — but among your own acquaintances, — and family?"

"As it happens, I've never been in London before; and I never remember any kith and kin, except a brother, and he, poor fellow, met his death the year I went abroad, — let me see, that was in the spring of '68."

Scott, apparently busy searching for something among the many papers that littered his desk, was in reality listening with strained attention.

"Your brother was older than you?" he hazarded.

"Michael was some five years my elder. He would be five-and-forty or so now. Excuse the question, but is anything the matter with you?"

Scott had gone white as the paper he held in his hand, that fluttered with the tremor of his pulse.

"Nothing," he said, with an effort; "nothing at all but this pain — ah! — it often takes me like this. Go on; what were you telling me?"

"I was speaking of my brother. He was a clever fellow. Had he lived, life would have gone very differently with me. As it is, the early mechanical training I had with him, — he was an engineer, — served me in good stead at Van Hannens', and so has been the indirect means of my obtaining an introduction to you."

"If you had a footing in their works, you could not have done better than held on. Theirs is a fine business; my operations are mere trifles in comparison."

Scott leaned his head on his hand, and traced abstractedly dots and dashes on the blotting-pad before him.

"But I had to get back to England," explained his visitor. "For many years my whole thoughts have been centred on getting back, and, strange as it may seem, I have never until now been able to manage it. Once I actually took ship, to be wrecked for the second time in my life; and on another occasion I got knocked on the head for the sake of my passage money. I spent the next two months in hospital, and the next two years hunting down the man who did it. I paid him back with interest," said O'Brien, grimly, "for I never forget a debt, — an idiosyncrasy that has injured me more than once. I had, for instance, many chances of settling down in America, could I have foregone my purpose of returning over here. But there are some things even dearer to a man than success."

"Yes, yes," said Scott, "peace of mind is best of all." His own peace was gone, — years ago, — but he was overcome now by unusual agitation. "Strange!" he mused, "strange that Michael should have a brother, and I not know it; stranger still that among all the millions in London, chance should lead that brother to me. But is it not Providence rather than chance who thus provides me with a means of making reparation? And even if I am mistaken, — yet the name? the date? no, I cannot be, — but even so, I will still help him for his own sake;" for Scott felt that inward leaning towards the stranger that comes to us when we first meet a person whom we shall afterwards call friend.

"Well, Mr. O'Brien," he said aloud, "I will see what I can do for you. Leave me your address, or perhaps you would n't mind giving me another call towards the end of the week? Saturday, shall we say? Yes; perhaps by that time I may have hit on something for you."

The visitor rose and took his departure; and he might possibly have looked more elated had he known into what good hands his interests were confided.

II.

SCOTT's thoughts that night dwelt persistently on the past. He had escorted his daughter Catherine to an evening party, and for the first time he had observed in her behavior a reminiscence of her dead mother's. The sight filled him with inexpressible pain. He could no longer look at her; he wandered through the hot gas-lighted rooms alone, examining the drawings on the walls, which he knew by heart these many years, and turning over the equally well-known albums of photographs on the side-tables.

While it was yet early he asked Catherine to come away, and she, always eager to please him, at once sought her wraps. Rolled cosily round in them, she leaned back in her corner of the carriage and rehearsed in smiling silence the scene she had just left.

Scott, usually so equable of temper, betrayed signs of annoyance. He let down the window nearest him with an unnecessary rattle; he stopped Catherine's fan in its progress of slipping off the front seat with an impatient word; finally, he glanced at the pretty, dreamy face beside him, and it seemed to add the last straw to his burden of discontent.

Catherine, returning his gaze, thought he looked tired, and was filled with self-reproach.

"You are feeling less well?" she said anxiously. "Oh, we ought not to have gone! I ought to have stayed at home quietly with you. I am a selfish wretch!"

"No, I'm all right," answered Scott; "it's not that. It's something else. You have enjoyed yourself, Catherine?"

"Very much indeed!" she answered, slightly surprised by his tone.

"I saw it!" cried he petulantly; "every one in the room could see it. You laughed and talked more than I have ever known you. You looked different — you look different now from your usual self."

Catherine leaned forward, love and apprehension blent in her beautiful eyes.

"Did I do anything wrong? or say anything? was anything the matter with my dress?"

"No; you looked very well, and you knew it. You betrayed your consciousness in every movement, in every tone. It was painful to me to be near you. A vain, coquettish woman is a terror to me."

Catherine was too startled to speak. She pressed her hands together in perplexity, and her cloak slipped from her bare arms. Scott drew it up again with tender care. His ebullition of temper had relieved him.

"I do not mean to accuse you of wilful coquetry; but you are young, dearest, and thoughtless. And you, too, have received the best gift that can come to a woman, if rightly used, — beauty. For God's sake, do not turn it to the sorrow, the desperation, perhaps, — who knows? — to the eternal loss of one of your fellow-creatures!"

Catherine was tongue-tied by the terrible earnestness of these words, as well as by the strangeness of any reproof from the most indulgent of friends and fathers.

"There were two young fellows there to-night," pursued Scott, "whom I have long supposed to be interested in you, who stand, I think, on the brink of a warmer feeling. I watched your conduct with them. You distributed kind words and smiles to each. You let Murchinson fan you, but you dropped your handkerchief for Hervey to pick up."

Catherine relapsed into smiles.

"Oh, no, I did not drop it on purpose!" she explained.

"You allowed Hervey to turn over the pages of your music, but you asked Murchinson to choose the song you should sing; and though it was his arm you accepted to the carriage, it was to Hervey you gave from the window your last good-bye."

"But how is that wrong?" asked Catherine, still smiling; "should I not try to be equally nice to them both?"

The cloak began to slip down once more, for her warm little hand had sought her father's, and crept inside it like a bird to its nest.

"How cold your hand is!" she said, shivering.

Scott's fingers closed over hers, at first fondly, then with unconscious force, until beneath the unendurable pressure she gave a cry of pain.

"Equally kind to them both?" he repeated; "don't you see what you are doing? You are encouraging both to hope where you can only satisfy one. They used to be friends; now on your account they are so no longer. I even see them exchange glances of enmity. If Hervey enjoys a momentary pre-eminence, Murchinson is cast down; if you accord Murchinson a favor, Hervey bites his lip and scowls. Always together when you are present, they avoid each other when alone. I heard Murchinson just now say to his friend, 'Are you going to walk?' and when he got the answer 'Yes,' then 'I'll ride,' said he, and turned on his heel. Formerly, as you remember, each enjoyed nothing so much as the other's company; but jealousy is a plant of rapid growth. Beginning with petty insults of this sort between comrades, no one can say to what it may not lead, — to the bitter word, the unforgivable blow, even to the crime of Cain."

It was here that Scott in his vehemence crushed Catherine's hand and wrung from her a cry.

"My poor darling, I have hurt you!" said he remorsefully, and carrying her fingers to his lips, he covered them with kisses. "There, I will not forget again what a delicate little hand it is. You know I would not purposely hurt it for the world."

"And I," said Catherine, with tears in her eyes, but again smiling, "did not mean to do the harm I appear to have done to-night. But it never occurred to me things were so serious, — even now, — oh, I feel sure neither of them cares for me in the way you mean."

"Perhaps not; perhaps I am mistaken. And yet, Catherine, let us imagine they do care, that both are anxious for your favor. Do you act fairly by them, in letting each one think you like him the best, or at least quite as well as the other?"

"Why, dearest," cried Catherine, laughing, "even if I did care for one in particular, which I don't, I should be bound to conceal it. You know a girl must not show preferences."

"Error, error," said Scott. "Is not a girl a human being too? Shall she not have her likes and dislikes with the rest of us? That is a fatal doctrine which teaches her to conceal every hint of the truth. My little daughter, I have known a case in which this unnatural reticence, due partly to a narrow education, partly to a cruel coquetry, worked irretrievable harm."

He paused, deep in thought. The image of another Catherine rose before him. He followed her through her brief career, down to the dreadful grave. There, one cold, wet day, long ago, he had left her who had so loved the sunshine and the light; but the sin, the anguish, the unavailing regret had remained with him ever since.

"A man," said he, presently, "will accept his fate manfully from the woman he loves, so long as she deals openly and honestly with him; but while she lures him on, he will cede to no one. Therefore, Catherine, I implore you to act frankly with those two young fellows. If there is one you like better than the other, do not be afraid to reveal it. Why should you be afraid? If he is poor, I have enough for you both; and why should I ask for family or position? I rose from the people myself. All I ask is that you should be happy and good, and make, through your affection, the man you marry good and happy likewise."

"It is evident I don't make you happy," said Catherine, playfully; "or you would not be so anxious to get rid of me."

"Should I not be the selfish wretch you called yourself just now, if I tried to keep you from the man you loved?"

"So you are making out it is I who am in

love now, sir?" cried Catherine, with reproach. "For the future, instead of being equally kind to every one, I must be equally cold."

"No; there is another danger there," said Scott; "young men have feelings as well as girls, and some are too shy, and some too proud, to fall in love without receiving any encouragement. I want you to let your heart lead you; then you cannot go wrong. And it is natural I should have anxieties about your future. Who knows how long I shall be here to take care of you?"

Time after time he said a word of this sort, with the design of gently preparing Catherine for the coming change. But the girl could not understand his meaning. His fits of pain, his lassitude, his visits to the physician, appeared to her only in connection with some passing indisposition, perhaps incidental to his great age.

She nestled close up to him.

"You are never going to leave me, dearest, and I am never going to marry. I am going to remain with you, and be your own little girl always."

The carriage reached home, and Scott, lifting his daughter out, pressed her gratefully in his arms; but he knew that, in spite of her innocent protestations, the day would come when she would think otherwise. And he would have hastened the moment had he been able, because, ever drawing nearer and more near, he foresaw for his darling the dark and lonely days of a first great grief.

III.

THE interest O'Brien aroused in Scott increased the more he saw of him. Eventually he made him a place in his own business, and found no occasion to regret having done so. O'Brien's new position threw him a good deal in Scott's society, who before long was addressing him with the familiarity of at least an old acquaintance. He even asked him to Streatham to dine, — an unusual token of favor, — and drove him out there on the following Saturday. The clerks, gayly preparing to close their week's work, and get away to their amusements, had crowded to the window to see the two gentlemen start. They remarked to each other how jolly old the "governor" looked.

In fact, Scott grew visibly older every day.

Any one would have said, offhand, he was sixty;
yet in reality he was not many years senior to
the man beside him. But O'Brien's upright
bearing, and broad shoulders, made Scott appear more than usually aged and infirm.

His residence, forty minutes' drive from the
city, stood back from the high road, in its own
pleasant grounds. Within the oak gates, a
gravel-sweep led to the house, which was low
and unpretending; yet to the discerning eyes
its well-kept approaches, its spruce exterior,
spoke of substantial wealth, which was con-
firmed by a first glance within. Here were
good pictures, soft carpets, handsome furniture;
all the innumerable indications that comfort is
understood and money plentiful. Well-trained,
attentive servants came to take the visitor's
coat and stick, and receive Scott's orders.
O'Brien looked about him with dark envy. It
was the most luxurious house he had ever been
in. For the first time in his life he walked
over tiger skins and tessellated pavements; he
saw decorations on the walls, and objects for
daily use which he had previously only associated with the stage. He tried to realize how
the possession of all these good things would
affect him, and he contrasted Scott's evident

ease with his own hardships and toil. He was filled with wrath.

The large drawing-room into which his host led him was empty. Scott passed out through a conservatory at the back, and thence down a semi-circular flight of stone steps on to the lawn. O'Brien saw a green, delightful solitude stretching round him. Stately trees cast their shadow over the grass, there was the tinkle of an unseen fountain, and the limits of the garden were cleverly concealed. It was an ideal place in which to spend long summer days of indolence.

Through the leafy screen on the right a gleam of white appeared and vanished. Then a girl in a white gown emerged from a side path and advanced towards them. She appeared about eighteen years of age, had a skin of milk and roses, gentlest of blue eyes, and quantities of fair hair wound round a well-poised little head. She carried a basket of ferns and flowers, green and white and scarlet.

O'Brien broke off short in the middle of a sentence, his gaze riveted upon her. The proud father understood his surprise and admiration. New acquaintances were invariably surprised at finding he possessed, hidden away in his home, so sweet a creature as Catherine.

"My daughter," said Scott fondly, as O'Brien turned towards him with impatient inquiry in his eyes; "Catherine, Mr. O'Brien."

"I am glad to see you," said Catherine, with timid hospitality, as she held out a little hand.

"I am glad to come," he answered, and then suddenly and oddly turned from her to study the scene.

"You have a charming place here," he remarked to her presently; "it has a pleasant, old-world air, very refreshing to a weary traveller like myself. I suppose you have lived here all your life?"

"As long as I can remember." said Catherine; "we came when I was quite a child, sixteen years ago."

"When her mother died," explained Scott, in the lowered tone in which a man mentions the still-loved dead; "the first four years of my marriage I had a cottage Hampstead way."

"Sixteen years," repeated O'Brien. "That is a long and enviable time to have spent in such an oasis as this; for it seems to me that life here must be always smooth and happy."

"Yes, yes," said Scott; "and if happiness were intended to be our portion on earth, under conditions similar to these, it might perhaps be attained." He looked from Catherine to the velvet lawns and pastures, to the low house, with its friendly aspect, and sun-awnings of white and red. "But it has not been so willed for man, and we have each of us to bear our cross."

"True," assented O'Brien; "there is no rose without its thorns; yet to one who has been so long the sport of chance as I have, ten years, five even, of such a peaceful home-life, would go a long way towards compensation. After that, I fancy I could face death without grumbling; but as it is, I should rebel, for it would seem hard to go without having tasted one of the good gifts for which life was given."

"Life was given for one thing only," said Scott, as though speaking to himself; "everything else passes as quickly as those shadows over the grass. Inequalities here will be set right in the world to come; and some of those who stand highest now will take the lowest places then, — if, indeed," he added, with passionate earnestness, "if, indeed, they find a place at all."

Catherine saw her father had entered into one of his religious reveries, which often made him oblivious to external things. To conceal his condition from strange, and perhaps unsympathizing eyes, she conquered her shyness sufficiently to ask O'Brien if he would care to go round the garden. She led him from point to point; showed him the great guelder rose-bush, with its million blossoms; the little fountain, where the goldfishes swam under a glittering cascade poured over them by a smiling Nereid, and the "turn-about" house, set on a pivot, so that a touch would bring it round to follow the sunshine; and he listened to her in such silence, and with such evident pre-occupation, that she might have thought he had forgotten all about her, but for the strangely intense look she encountered if she chanced to meet his eye.

Presently he abandoned taciturnity and began to talk. She had taken him into the orchid-house to exhibit with especial pride her favorite flowers. He told her of the countries where he had seen these growing wild, common as weeds.

"You have travelled a great deal, my father tells me," said Catherine.

"Yes, I have been a rolling stone, and consequently have gathered no moss; so that I find myself, Miss Scott, at an age when other men have homes and children, about to begin life over again. I am absolutely no further advanced than I was twenty years ago."

"Oh, but you have been unlucky," said Catherine, gently. "Now that you are home in England you will find things will go better."

She blushed at her temerity in offering these timid consolations, and O'Brien watched her furtively.

"Yes, I think the luck has changed now," he answered. "I see the goal plainly at last." But his manner was still charged with gloom.

Catherine was puzzled. His long dark glances confused her. She was glad that the gong at that moment recalled them to the house.

At dinner the conversation turned upon the guest's travels. Scott, whose life was so uniform, who knew no greater excitement than the rise and fall of markets, no greater danger than the crossing of Leadenhall Street, was much interested in the other's strange tales. O'Brien warmed to his work. He shook off his moroseness, and without either boasting or self-depreciation, set forth his adventures in manly fashion, selecting episodes he thought most likely to interest, and painting lively pictures of foreign life and manners.

Catherine listened enthralled. Never had any one, within her limited experience, spoken like this, seen so many marvels, or done such courageous things. In her heart she appraised at their just value the deeds he passed so lightly by. Her cheeks glowed; her sweet eyes involuntarily expressed her homage. Yet she did not know the full meaning of the new emotions awakening within her breast; and, had she been asked with what sentiment O'Brien most inspired her, she would undoubtedly have told you with fear. For, though it pleased her so much to hear him talk, she could scarcely answer for rising blushes and fluttering pulse.

IV.

O'BRIEN began to come over to Streatham at regular and frequent intervals. It seemed to Scott his guest took pleasure in walking about the gardens with Catherine, in telling his stories to her gentle ear. It was while watching them thus together one day that the idea first presented itself to Scott's mind that, by giving his daughter to James O'Brien, he should be making the best and fittest atonement. For he no longer felt the smallest doubt that this man, led by chance across his path, had, all unknown to O'Brien himself, the strongest possible claim upon him. And even for Catherine's own sake, it seemed such a marriage might be best. In O'Brien she would find a more indulgent husband than in a younger man. Young men, said Scott to himself, are often selfish and tyrannical; such a one might make Catherine's life a slavery. But O'Brien would know how to value the gift, and to unite the tenderness of a father with the ardor of a lover. He was more than twenty years her senior, and yet, in appearance, still young, — upright, well-built, and possessing a face and mien of which any woman might be proud.

Now, as he walked by Catherine's side across the lawn, he looked particularly well. With her he put off some of his gloom, and bending down towards her as he talked, — for the top of her head was but just on a level with his shoulder, — he called forth constantly on her charming little face the most responsive smiles and dimples.

It seemed to Scott that so far as Catherine was concerned, his wishes would meet with no resistance. And he did begin to wish this thing earnestly. He not only liked O'Brien as much as he had liked only one other man in his life, but he believed that Providence was thus offering him a means of expiation for the past. O'Brien should marry Catherine, succeed to the business, and then money, house, all Scott possessed, should be given to her and to him.

It was a happy spring and summer for David Scott, happier than any he had lived through for the last twenty years. Though he suffered much physical pain, his anxieties were less, and the burden of remorse which weighed down his soul began to lift.

Catherine, too, was filled with a new life, or, rather, life seemed to hold a new meaning for her. All smiles and blushes when O'Brien was present, she rippled over with happiness when alone. She sang as she ran up and down stairs, or as she wandered through the quiet garden. Murchinson and Hervey were completely forgotten.

O'Brien had more than once made casual allusion to that private business which had mainly brought him to London, and Scott had felt such curiosity as may be pardoned when it springs from a desire to serve. One evening, as the three were sitting on the lawn after dinner, it recurrred to him again, this business, and he wondered whether it was such as might offer any impediment to his hopeful castle building.

O'Brien smoked in silence, and Catherine watched the stars, trooping forth in myriads upon the darkening summer sky.

"By-the-by," remarked Scott, tentatively, "that affair of yours, you have once or twice alluded to, — I hope it is progressing satisfactorily?"

O'Brien looked up abruptly at the first word; then he threw away his cigar, though it was but half burned out, and turned his chair to fully face Scott.

"Circumstances are combining to favor me," he said, "better than I ever dreamed possible; and after twenty years' patience, I seem on the verge of attaining my heart's desire." He paused — a long, intolerable pause it seemed to Scott — before he added, "Justice to a criminal, and vengeance for a crime."

Catherine too had begun to listen the moment O'Brien began to speak. Already sensitive to every change in his voice, her eyes opened in terror at the ferocity of his tone.

"You think I speak vindictively, Miss Scott?" he asked her. "I *am* vindictive, — it runs in my Irish blood. We love and hate warmly and forever; and there is a man to whom I owe a debt of hatred hard to pay."

Scott leaned forward with interest.

"What was this crime?" said he.

"Murder," came the curt answer. "And the victim was my only brother, Michael O'Brien."

It had grown almost too dark for the men to distinguish each other's faces, but Catherine cried out with indignation —

"Oh, your brother! How wicked!" And the murderer at that moment would have found scant mercy at her hands.

"Yes, it was a cruel piece of work," began O'Brien; "for this man and poor Michael were friends. Yet he murdered him, and spread the report that Michael, in a fit of caprice, had joined an outward-bound ship and sailed for America."

"But how did the murderer escape if you knew of the crime?" asked Scott from his dusky corner.

"The story is rather singular. I made the discovery in this way. One day I was taking a lonely ramble along the shore — this occurred down at Hardsmouth, the cliffs on either side of the town rise abruptly, and the coast is solitary and dangerous — but perhaps you may know those parts?"

"I do," said Scott; "I was there on business some six years since."

"Well, I was rambling about there one day some months after Michael's disappearance — I should explain I had come purposely up from the south to join my brother in business, only to find to my surprise and grief he had gone abroad, so it was told me — I was wandering along the shore disconsolately enough, when, rounding a promontory, I was surprised to find the little cove beyond full of crows, either walking over the sands or flying heavily in the air. Disturbed at my approach, they rose and settled on a jutting-out portion of rock, some twenty or thirty feet above my head. There, wedged into a cleft, I saw what appeared to be a bundle of old clothes. Boylike, I must climb to discover what this might mean. I shouted to scare the birds away. They flapped their ugly wings in circles round my head.

Something sickening hung out from the bundle. It was a half-eaten and decaying human hand, the flesh hanging in tatters, the bones showing."

"Oh," murmured Catherine, "how dreadful!"

"In a few seconds more I discovered to what this ghastly relic belonged. The bundle of clothes concealed the body of poor Michael, whom I had last seen six months before, full of life and vigor, whom I had loved, who was the only relation I had in the world."

"That was a terrible discovery," said Scott, sympathetically; "yet what leads you to suppose it was a murder? Might not your brother have met with a misadventure? The cliffs round Hardsmouth are notoriously dangerous, and on a dark night a man walking along the top might easily miss his footing and be blown over."

"Such was my own impression at first; but as I lay there upon the rock, innumerable scraps of evidence presented themselves to my mind, which together convinced me it was the work of a murderer. It would not interest you to hear all the details by which I roughly arrived at the theory which I have since elaborated during many years of painful retrospect.

This man, this friend of Michael's, had a cause for hating him. Perhaps Michael had won the affections of some girl the other coveted, for my brother, as I remember him, Miss Scott, was a most gay and lovable fellow, — as different as possible from the man you see me. Perhaps thereupon the false friend laid a trap to entice Michael along the edge of the cliff at night, and then, suddenly springing upon him unawares, flung him over. He trusted to the solitary nature of the spot to keep his secret, — for twenty years ago the coast down there was still more sparsely inhabited than it is at present, — and, but for that chance walk of mine, the remains might never have been found until they were past recognition."

"Human nature is vile," said Scott; "no one knows better than I how deeply man may fall, but such cold-blooded treachery as you describe this man guilty of, I am loath to believe in. Is it not more probable to suppose the two may have quarrelled, come to blows, and then perhaps — "

"My brother have fallen over accidentally?" said O'Brien, concluding the sentence. "No; had it been accidental, and the men struggling,

THE EXPIATION OF DAVID SCOTT.

both must have gone over together, and if one saw the danger in time to save himself, he could have saved his friend. Besides, the report so sedulously spread of the victim's departure for foreign parts proves conclusively the guilt of him who spread it."

"But what did you do?" asked Catherine eagerly.

"At this point my own adventures begin. I hung there, clinging on to the rock, and turning things over in my mind, when a boat came in sight a few yards from the shore. I hailed the three men who were in her, and who at first seemed little disposed to stop; but, after consulting together, they turned her head and ran her up the beach. I made haste to tell them my story; they appeared friendly, advised me to leave the body precisely as I had found it, and to go with them and lay an information before the magistrates. I got into the boat, and they pulled for the harbor; it was already past sundown, and the evening was quite closed in before we reached the bar. Here, lying in the offing, all ready for sailing, was a Portuguese trading-vessel, and aboard her, by some easy excuse or other, my companions managed to decoy me. But no sooner was my foot set on deck than I received a knock-down blow, and recovered consciousness only to find myself out at sea, with my choice of supplementing the wretchedly incompetent crew or tasting the cat. We were bound for Loanga, but never reached our destination, as we were wrecked off the coast of Dahomey. There I fell into the hands of the blacks, and lived in slavery for five years. Slavery is not a condition to soften the heart, and it was then, Miss Scott, I made up my mind to outlive any suffering — and I endured many — for the pleasure of one day taking my revenge."

"Vengeance," said Scott, in a low voice, "belongs to the Lord. Be sure in His own time He will repay, ay, full measure and running over."

"Yes," agreed O'Brien; "but even you good people admit the Lord helps those most who help themselves. I will help myself here. Think of my brother's terrible and lingering death; for it is evident he was not killed outright by the fall, but got fixed there in the rock, to die of loss of blood or of starvation. Think of what I have gone through since. We have each of us but one life given us, and the man took Michael's, and for twenty years has

THE EXPIATION OF DAVID SCOTT. 273

rendered mine exceeding bitter. The Lord may do as He pleases with his soul hereafter, but I think I have every right to demand satisfaction from him here."

"Catherine," said her father, tenderly, "it is getting chilly; it is time you should go in."

"It is time we should all go in," added O'Brien. "I must be getting away."

Scott accompanied him to the door to bid him good-night.

O'Brien produced a pipe from his pocket and set about lighting it; but he was awkward with the matches, which went out one after the other. Meanwhile he spoke musingly: —

"The O'Briens," said he, "may be found every hour of the day, in every quarter of the globe; but I suppose the name of David Scott is not so very unusual either?"

"The combination is about as common as any you will find," said the host.

"Ah!" O'Brien struck the fourth match successfully; it flared up, so that for an instant both men's faces were visible in the glow. "Curiously enough the man who murdered my poor Michael, and whom I have been seeking these many years past, was also named David Scott."

V.

Scott passed the night walking up and down his bedroom unintermittingly but softly, so as not to awaken Catherine in the adjoining room.

His thoughts went back to the days when the dead and more dearly-loved Catherine was alive and young. He lived over again a certain evening, when Catherine Eames, seventeen, and radiantly pretty, was radiantly happy likewise; for her two lovers had come up to supper, and it was easy to see from the dark glances and bitter speeches that passed between them, how jealous each was of the other, and how much both aspired to her favor.

Catherine did all she could to foment their bad feeling. If she gave David a sweet smile, she straightway touched Michael's hand by accident as she dispensed her hospitality; if she laughed one moment at Michael's half-malicious jests, the next she had turned to David, and with pretty pleading eyebrows and bewitching ways, knew how without a word to get her laughter pardoned.

The unfortunate young men suffered torments; but instead of tracing the origin of their pain to Catherine, where it was due, and putting a stop once for all to her thoughtless cruelty, they turned fiercely on each other, and their old friendship was half burned up in the fires of their new passion.

Catherine's father, stolid, phlegmatic, indifferent to everything but his supper and his doze, ate and slept the evening away, and noticed nothing of the young people's folly.

"You will both come again and see me in three weeks' time," said Catherine, "when I shall be back from auntie's? and then — perhaps — I may — " She paused to smile coquettishly at one and the other.

"Then you will give us your answer?" implored David. "You will decide between us, Catherine?"

Michael listened, and laughed; he played tunes with his fingers on the supper-cloth, and tried to inform David by his whole demeanor that the decision held small terrors for him personally; but when Catherine turned towards him he immediately dropped his boastful air, and became once more the devout lover.

"Perhaps I shall never come back at all," said Catherine, merely to tease. "Who knows if I may not meet my fate down there?"

The wild, gusty December wind rushed at the cottage, and shook every door and window with violence, as though seeking to force an entrance; the log-fire crackled gloriously up the chimney, and red reflections played over the cosey house-place and its four occupants, — upon Eames, who, with folded hands and head fallen back, dreamed uneasily of business complications and vanishing joints of roast; upon Catherine, turning her fair hair to gold, her eyes to jewels, her flushing cheek and tiny ear to sunset-clouds, to sea-shells, or to anything else that might seem appropriate to the poetical fancy of the lover; finally, it glowed warmly over the two young men with all the impartiality of Catherine herself. It contrasted Michael's handsome Irish face with David's northern fairness, and so enhanced and equalized the good looks of both, that in point of beauty alone it was impossible to decide which deserved the preference. The stormy wind, rattling at the door, mingled with Catherine's light words, and set Michael quoting:—

"'Fate and fortune come without knocking,'" said he. "Give us your answer candidly to-night, Catherine; for who can tell if in three weeks' time we shall be here to receive it? *You*, as you say, may stop down there at your aunt's altogether, or a sudden whim may seize *me* to take ship to the antipodes, and never be heard of again."

"In that case," cried Catherine, "my answer can be of no importance to you."

"Oh, it would be something to meditate on in the watches of the night!" he answered, and his blue eyes drew hers and held them fixed for one pensive moment upon his own. A deeper color came to her cheek.

"Have you nothing to meditate on without that?" she asked him, smiling; and Michael thrust a careless hand into his breast.

"Ah, to be sure! There are plenty of nice girls down at Hardsmouth," he said. "I will meditate upon Maggie or on Liz."

Catherine's smile only broadened, and David, forever on the watch, turned pale. Just now it appeared to him there had passed a glance of secret understanding between the two. He looked darkly at Catherine, who turned towards him a face of child-like innocence; he looked at his friend, but found no more in Michael's triumphant expression than he was well used to. Michael was always sanguine; up to the very brink of disaster, his Celtic impetuosity knew no check, his self-confidence was never one whit abated. He lived gayly in the present moment, with neither regret for the past nor fears for the future.

David took life more seriously; he was of a religious turn of mind. He ardently desired to save his soul, but he likewise framed plans to conquer Fortune. Lately, Catherine had become the centre and source of all his daydreaming, and he thought even more of winning her for his wife, than of making money or obtaining grace. His worldly position was better than Michael's, and he believed he should have the old man's good word.

The last mad wind-whirl had disturbed Eames, and his comfortless position in the chair, on the top of a plentiful meal, had given him nightmare. He awoke with a groan, sat up, and saw Catherine and the boys still siting as he had left them at the supper-table, although they had long since finished. Michael was building up a pyramid of knives and glasses. Catherine watched the structure as it rose, and David looked at Catherine. Presently she put out a mischievous hand to interfere, but Michael, still building with his right, caught her wrist in his left hand, and held it fast. With an impatient jerk of the table, David brought the edifice crashing down in ruins.

"If you break the glasses," said Eames, "you'll get no hot toddy. Cathey, it's time you were abed; get out the whiskey and mix the boys a glass apiece, and your poor old father will have one too."

Catherine fetched the bottle, the lemons, and the old-fashioned silver sugar-crushers. Michael pared the peel into strips so thin "you might read through them," and David lifted the kettle, too heavy for the girl's slender arms. The fragrant odor of punch spread about the room, and the young men clinked glasses with Eames and drank to their next meeting.

"You've got a rough walk before you, boys," said he; "I shouldn't care to be in your place. But, to be sure, you're young; your united ages don't come up to mine, I'll be bound. Let me see, — you're twenty-three, Michael, and David's twenty-five. Twenty and twenty is forty, and five and three is eight. Add another five to forty-eight, and there you have me. Well, twenty years goes by like a flash, as one day you'll discover for yourselves."

He pressed the young men to take just another half-glass. "A warm inside keeps the cold without," said he, dealing forth the spirit generously.

They were glad to delay the moment of departure, and Catherine coquetted to the last. She handed David his comforter and laughed at the fashion in which Michael wore his.

"You've tied it very badly, all the ends are hanging out. Let me do it for you."

Standing on tip-toes, her head just reached to Michael's chin. She was unnecessarily long in her arrangements, and when she had finished she turned her charming little face upwards, with something so provocative in her baby eyes, that no young mortal Irishman, especially after Eames's hospitality, could resist doing as Michael did, and suddenly kissing her.

David turned white.

"Early times for kissing," grumbled Eames.

"No, late times," said Catherine; "I am saying good-night." With woman's wit she held her blushing cheek up to her father and David in turn, as if it were but ordinary friendliness.

David was red enough now, as he awkwardly took the kiss she proffered him.

Michael made a grimace.

"You know how to cheapen your favors," he told Catherine, who blushed still deeper, but answered pertly, "It will be a long time before you obtain such another favor anyhow."

The whole party went out into the porch, and David opened the outer door. The wind drove him back an instant as it rushed triumphantly past him, lifting the carpet from the boards, blowing the curtains into strange suggestive shapes, finally losing itself in the great roaring cavern of a chimney.

Outside, up in the domed heavens, a gibbous moon, now visible, now hidden, climbed swiftly through the drifting clouds. The scene was alternately washed in cold white light or plunged in blackness, and the suddenness and completeness of these changes was full of an eerie desolation.

"Good-night," said Eames to the young men.

"Good-night!" they cried, setting off.

"Good-night, Davy," said Catherine, in her most caressing tone, and making use for the first time that evening of the familiar diminutive. "Good-night, Michael."

Both turned back and waved their caps with

a final "good-night." All four saw each other for the last time in the wan moonlight, then Eames pulled his daughter within doors, and the two friends trudged on together.

They went without speaking a mile along their road. The last house of the village was left behind, as, striking across the meadows, they reached the cliff, along the ragged outline of which their route lay. The moon began to disentangle herself from the vaporous meshes that held her; she reached a breadth of dark transparent sky, and for a time shone out unimpeded and strong. Every leaf and blade of grass became suddenly distinguishable upon the clifftop; every bright ripple crest and dark hollow might be counted on the sheet of silver sea that crawled below.

David, since he parted from Catherine, had not opened his lips. The look he still believed he had surprised between her and Michael rankled within him. His blood was on fire with the kiss she had let him take; perhaps too Eames's whiskey counted for something. He said to himself over and over again, Catherine should be his, and the annoying conviction pressed close upon him, that but for Michael there was no one in the world to dispute his claim.

Michael, who had not spoken either, was yet never silent. Now he whistled, now he hummed under his breath, now he sang a few bars out loud. All at once he laughed outright.

David felt a passionate resentment.

"What a fool you are!" he exclaimed savagely, "everything to you is a matter for jest. Yet the very next time we walk along here together, Catherine will have made her choice, and one of us will be the happiest fellow in the world, one the most miserable."

"Perhaps I am cultivating a laughing philosophy," replied Michael, "in order to enable me to sustain my fate, and yet —"

"Yet what?" repeated David.

"Well, of course we each hope to have the luck," said Michael, apologetically, "and I cannot help being gay-hearted while such a hope is mine."

The mere possibility that his rival should succeed and he fail, cut David like a knife, but he marshalled up all the facts that told in his favor, and found relief.

"Even supposing," said he, "Catherine cared for you, what then? How could you support her as a wife? You have only just enough to live yourself. Do you mean to ask her to wait for you? Eames would not consent. He's a shrewd man. He understands business. I talked with him to-day for a long time. I let him know my position and my prospects. He was pleased. I am almost sure I can count upon his influence. In fact he hinted as much. He said he wanted a son-in-law competent to put Catherine's own little bit of money to good use."

Michael laughed again.

"You are a canny Scot, Davy," said he, "and where money is concerned you're bound to win. But while you were getting round old Eames, I for once was better employed. I was in the kitchen helping Catherine make the pies. I sat on a corner of the table and handed her the pepper, salt, and herbs as she wanted them. Do you know she is different when you're alone with her? She's gentler, and doesn't make fun of what you say."

There was a rapturous expression on Michael's face that told his companion, plain as words could, he was living over again his hour with Catherine in the kitchen.

"Have you ever noticed her ear?" he went on; "I didn't know an ear could be such a beautiful thing. It's so small and so perfect.

I wonder how any man could have been such a brute as to bore that little hole through it! She says it did n't hurt her much, but imagine hurting her at all!"

Every word wrenched the knife round in David's heart; every moment his face grew more fixed and bloodless. Unconscious or careless of the effect he was producing, Michael went on: "There's a wonderful down over her cheek, though you only see it when she turns against the light. It is like the bloom on fruit, you would almost fear to brush it away with a breath. It must feel like velvet to the finger. Then her hands. How horny Eames's are, and ours too. Look at that." Michael held out a large palm roughened and engrained by weather and work.

"But Catherine's is quite soft and pink, and is crossed inside by hundreds of funny little lines, like a crumpled poppy leaf before it's shaken out of the husk. And it's so small! She measured it against mine, and it lay here in the centre like a child's. The tips of her fingers don't reach to this;" and he drew an imaginary line across his first finger-joints.

David stood still, for his limbs were suddenly powerless; every drop of blood, all energy, had gone to feed the fury welling up in his heart.

"What right have you to know such things?" he demanded huskily; "what right have you to touch her? You desecrate her by your speech, by your thoughts. I have never so much as squeezed her hand, and you — did I not see you to-night put her to shame, by kissing her before us all?"

"You should be the last to complain of that, remembering what it earned you," Michael retorted. "But what I do before her father I dare not do behind his back. When alone with Catherine I am more timid, and go no further than she leads."

"I swear she never leads you!" cried David, violently; "you insult her by every word you say."

Michael did not seem to hear; he was immersed in pleasurable recollections.

"To-day her hair fell down all about her shoulders and below her waist. She had run into the garden to catch her kitten that had escaped, and the wind loosened it and blew it about like a yellow cloud. I wanted to take it in my hands, but I was afraid. I suppose she saw my longing in my face, for she got her scissors from her work-box and cut off for me a long thick piece. I have it here," and Michael thrust his hand into his breast.

David recalled the similar movement when Catherine had said to him, "Have you nothing else to meditate upon?" and he understood at last the look which they had exchanged. Michael had played him false. Three months ago they had agreed to court Catherine openly and in each other's presence, and to loyally accept her choice; but now Michael had tampered with her affection in an underhand manner, and had got her to concede to him unwarrantable favors.

Love, rage, and jealousy sent David, usually the most sensible of young men, clean off his head. He sprang upon Michael with the vague idea of tearing open his coat and proving him a liar, or else of wresting from him the lock of hair of which he made his boast. Michael, astonished at the attack, then angry too, struck back, and his blow falling upon his assailant's mouth laid the lip open, while his own knuckles streamed with blood. This was enough to change both men to wild beasts. They fought with fury, neither remembering nor caring for the cause. Locked in each other's arms, they swayed this way and that, and, oblivious of the danger, came every moment nearer to the cliff's edge. Both were strong, evenly matched in weight and height. David had a temporary advantage, having got Michael below him, but at the same moment he grew cognizant of their peril, and the shock sobered him at once. It was perhaps even then too late, they were already on the brink. The horror legible in his eyes caused Michael to glance round in his turn; down, down fell the precipice, almost perpendicularly to the shore. His grip upon David's arms, born of ferocity, tightened in despair.

"Back, David, for God's sake! . . . for Catherine's," he whispered hoarsely. But David felt, with agony of mind, the ground sliding away beneath him. Was there nothing on all this great round slippery earth by which to catch hold? His foot encountered an obstacle; with all his strength he held against the knotty root of some long-perished tree that laced the ground in his path. They were saved! But when Michael said "for Catherine's sake," David's feelings underwent another change. His hatred returned a thousand-fold; he no longer wished to save his rival, he wished to

THE EXPIATION OF DAVID SCOTT. 289

thrust him back, to leave him to his fate. Perhaps he did transmute this impulse into action; perhaps Michael must have fallen anyway. David never knew. All passed in a flash of lightning. With an uncertain cry, Michael crashed down to death alone, and David lay on the grass where he had fallen, and stared at the sky and the sailing moon, and vaguely calculated how soon she would reach that great bank of black cloud that yawned before her.

Next he observed on the grass, at a little distance from him, Michael's cap, which had fallen off in the struggle. He would have recognized it anywhere by its shape, its color, its frayed and sun-browned binding. The blustering wind racing along the cliff top raised the cap on edge, played with it capriciously, whirled it to the brink of the precipice, balanced it there, toppled it over.

David experienced horrible pain at seeing this senseless, inanimate object thus disappear before his eyes. It woke him from his stupor. It carried his thoughts down to Michael; he shuddered. Had he died quickly, or was he alive and conscious of the increeping sea, that within a few hours would wash high up the base of every rock and boulder along that lonely coast?

David crept along the edge, leaned over the abyss, called down with all his strength. The wind seized hold of his voice, scattered it hither and thither, overpowering it.

No human sound might reach to one down there below; vision might not scan the depth of those Titan walls, nor cleave the blackness of their shadows. Yet for a moment David, hanging over the precipice, fancied he could distinguish a dark and awful something blotting the moon-white shore; then the light flickered, paled, went out, the moon had reached the swarthy cloud bank, she passed into it and left him alone.

He got up and stumbled home through the windy darkness. As he went he rehearsed the three years of his good friendship with Michael. Closest, most inseparable of companions, never an unkind word had passed between them, until they had made the acquaintance of Catherine Eames. Now, because of this girl, Michael's body lay crushed at the foot of Browncap Cliff, and David was not only a murderer, but to conceal his crime must become a liar and a hypocrite as well.

He loathed himself; his old love for Michael was strong within him; and nevertheless, before the next sun rose, he had skilfully pieced together and learned by heart the story he was prepared to adhere to throughout the remainder of his life.

VI.

"What do you mean to do?"

This was the question Scott asked O'Brien the first moment he found himself alone with him next day. There was no doubt left in Scott's mind now but that O'Brien knew him for the murderer of his brother Michael.

"I have not come to a decision," answered O'Brien, with more than usual gloom.

"Did you know all along I was the man you were in search of?"

"When I heard of you from the Van Hannens, it occurred to me you might be the man; but when I saw you I fancied I was mistaken, you looked so much older than I expected."

"To bear a secret burden of guilt for twenty years does age a man," said Scott, humbly; "but for my poor Catherine's sake, I should be glad now the end has come."

This conversation took place in Scott's private office during an interval of business.

Within a few feet was the room full of pen-driving clerks, young fellows who now and then exchanged a gay jest over their work; beyond, again, was the jar and rumble of city life; all things ran in their accustomed grooves; only for Scott was the world revolutionized. His prosperous, honored, hypocritical career was at an end, and the question this morning of paramount importance to him, was how and when O'Brien meant to pluck away the mask.

"It was seeing your daughter convinced me I was on the right track," O'Brien told him; "she has her mother's name and her mother's hair."

Scott was astonished. "How can you know that?"

The other took from his breast-pocket an oblong packet. Unfolding the paper in which it was wrapped, he produced an old and shabby pocket-book.

"This was Michael's," said he. "I took it from the body that evening, and through all my wanderings and misadventures I have managed to keep it safe. Sea-water, time, and friction have rubbed away the writing it once contained, but long ago I learned its contents by heart. There, over and over again, stood a woman's name, 'Catherine,' 'Catherine Eames,' and sometimes 'Catherine O'Brien;' once it stood 'Catherine Scott,' but a black line had then been run through it. And here in the pocket I found a treasure time has not destroyed."

He laid upon the table a long tress of woman's hair, fine in texture, yellow in color, and wanting but the brightness of living hair to be the precise counterpart of Catherine Scott's.

It was the actual lock of hair for possessing which Michael had lost his life, and David had earned the curse of Cain. Tears came into Scott's eyes as he looked at this last memento of all the beauty that had gone to dust.

"It seems a small thing now to have quarrelled over," he said; "but then it meant to me so much. Yet if she had only told me . . . for after all she loved your brother best. I found this out when it was too late. But even from the very beginning the shadow of the dead stood between me and her, and when she lay dying, and I knelt beside her, it was his name she uttered with her failing breath. I never pray to God but Michael comes to appeal against me, and Catherine in heaven knows all, and turns away her face. At eight-and-twenty my hair was gray, and you see what I am now . . . broken up, a wreck. . . . What is it you mean to do?"

"I don't know," said the other, again. Deep furrows seamed themselves in his forehead, and he looked at Scott with rancorous eyes. Not because of Scott's crime against Michael, which he had long known, but because in his own breast a strange and enraging sentiment of pity warred with his legitimate revenge. The hopes of one day meeting with his brother's murderer, and exacting payment to the uttermost farthing, had lent him the energy and vitality to survive privations that would have killed another man; the idea had been to him a talisman of power which had over and over again brought him unharmed from the jaws of death. Yet now that the moment for which he had so long waited was come, he hesitated. In spite of all, he felt a friendship, an affection almost, for David Scott, that filled him with scorn for himself. He set about recalling his former feelings in the hopes of reanimating them.

"Often," said he aloud, "have I planned out in my exile what I should do when I met with Michael's murderer. I pictured to myself that if I should find him poor, obscure, uncared for, with nothing precious to him but his worthless life, then I would take that life, I would seize him by the throat, and, reminding him of Michael, slowly press his breath from him. But should I, on the contrary, find him as I have actually found you, rich, honored, well thought of, with loving hearts on which to lean, then I promised myself I would denounce him, drag him to justice, let him suffer all the torturing slowness of the law before expiating his crime by a shameful death. You think perhaps I have not sufficient proof? or that after so many years I could not obtain a conviction?"

"I should confess everything," answered Scott; "here and now, if you wish it, I will write a confession, and sign it before witnesses. How often have I not longed to unburden my soul, and lacked courage! You talk of punishment, of expiation; believe me, a man may suffer all the tortures of hell within his own heart. What cuts more sharply than unavailing regret?"

"The scorn of one's fellow-men," said O'Brien, calling up the dregs of his waning anger to give poignancy to his tone; "the child's knowledge that the father is unworthy of her honor and her love."

"Our sins shall be visited on our children," murmured Scott; "and yet . . . my poor Catherine, I would spare her if I could. Sometimes I hoped that God would permit me through her . . . to make you reparation?"

O'Brien's face became a dusky red, his eyes glowed; the next moment he was iron again, and had bitten back the words on the tip of his tongue.

"What I, myself, might have hoped for under other circumstances, has been rendered impossible by your crime. What connection could I have with the murderer of my brother? Would not his spirit haunt me? As it is, I am becoming contemptible to myself. I am temporizing and allowing human considerations to come between me and my just revenge."

"Do not let mistaken pity hold your hand. I am at your mercy. Show it by dealing the blow quickly. Suspense alone is more than I can bear."

"I shall choose my own time and my own measures," said O'Brien, malignantly, "and if you find the suspense hard, remember it is not one-tenth of the misery your victim suffered, dying on the rocks alone; or that I have gone through since, thanks to you. I have yet to consider the necessary steps to take, and I will let you know when I come to a decision."

A clerk here entered, introducing urgent business, and no more was said; but Scott tacitly accepted his enemy's conditions, and resumed his outward life of honorable composure.

It became apparent to Scott that if O'Brien had ever cared for Catherine, he had successfully crushed out the sentiment. Now, when he came over to Streatham, he avoided being alone with her. He sat in churlish silence. If she addressed him he did not seem to hear, or else answered her abruptly, even rudely; on which her pretty eyes would fill with tears, and for ten minutes after such a rebuff she could scarcely command herself to speak; then she would find excuses for him in her heart, feel sure the fault was hers, and try a thousand dear devices for making herself more pleasing. If he still neglected her, she would go to the piano and sing, and O'Brien found it difficult, when listening to her sweet young voice, to maintain his moroseness.

Scott watched her with admiration and pain. She was so like the other Catherine in face and form, so different in disposition. The other Catherine had accepted all homage as her right. This Catherine seemed to plead for kindness as a favor. The mother had played capriciously with the passionate hearts that loved her. The daughter, in retribution as it were, offered her fresh, intense affections to one who coldly turned aside.

O'Brien at length gave up visiting at Streatham at all. Catherine waited, hoped, grew anxious, and sought her father.

"Why does Mr. O'Brien no longer come here?" she asked; "is he ill?"

"No," Scott answered, "he was at the office to-day."

"Then why does he not come as he used to?"

"Perhaps he is busy."

"Oh, but not in the evening! Ask him, dearest, to come out to dinner to-morrow."

"Well, is he not coming?" was the first question she put, when her father returned alone the next day.

"My dear, he thanks you for the invitation, but he has another engagement."

It was misery to Scott to see how Catherine's color came and went, and how her eyes filled up with tears.

"It is I who stand in my darling's way," he thought. He began to wonder if his death would make any difference, whether then O'Brien would be able to forgive the girl her parentage. He began to watch with a new interest the progress of his disease.

Catherine could not sleep. She came down in the mornings looking pale and tired. Scott lay awake at night, too, but this was from the ever-increasing physical pain. Presently he was no longer able to go into business.

VII.

ONE day in September James O'Brien came over to Streatham. He had at last made up his mind what he should do, and he wished to communicate his intentions to David Scott.

He was shown into the study, where Scott lay back in an arm-chair supported by pillows. There was a great and ghastly change in his face. For this O'Brien had been prepared, partly by Scott's absence from the office, partly by a few words he had exchanged with a gentleman who was leaving the house, as O'Brien entered it. This was a minister of Scott's church; he had been sitting with the invalid. He spoke of Scott's great sufferings, and in conventional phraseology, but with real earnestness, of his Christian patience, and of the loss he would be to them all, if the Lord saw fit to take him. The servant joined in, to praise his master; and O'Brien's observant eye took stock of the inquiry cards that completely covered the hall-table. All these tokens of respect and solicitude awoke anew the devil in his breast, and he more than half regretted the resolution he had come to, which was to relinquish his vengeance and leave the murderer to fate. A variety of motives had brought him to this; principally, perhaps, the strange affection he felt for the man who had so injured him.

Scott, looking up at his visitor with deprecation, did not venture to offer his hand.

"It's very kind of you to come and see me," he said.

"I have come to tell you I am going away, back to America. You are safe. I have broken my vow." O'Brien refused a chair, and stood gazing moodily into the vacant garden.

"Why do you spare me?" asked Scott humbly.

"Because I'm a fool, I suppose, and a coward."

"But why do you go?" said Scott; "I shall not be here long, for do not think I shall escape punishment. The hand of God is upon me. It is hard to leave my poor Catherine all alone; and death itself is hard."

O'Brien looked about the room. There lay Catherine's little embroidered handkerchief on the open book, from which she had probably been reading aloud. Here, on the table by Scott's elbow, was a glorious bunch of purple grapes; the pillows behind his head, the shawl over his knees had been arranged by loving hands. O'Brien called to mind the sympathy of the minister, the eulogy of the servant, the cards from acquaintances and friends. He was filled with bitterness.

"Some deaths are harder than others," said he. "You find it hard to die here among your own people, waited on by those who love you, with every alleviation that money and science can give. You are attended by the first doctor in London, who, though he cannot cure you, can relieve your pain. Your clergyman comes and talks to you of God and of His forgiveness, and all who know you speak of you with respect and regret. All day long your daughter Catherine is by your side to soothe you with her caresses. You will pass away in her arms, death will lose half its terrors with your head reposing on her tender breast. And you call that expiation? Let me remind you how Michael died. Suddenly, in the midst of life and strength, he found himself face to face with death. And it was a cruel and lingering death to which he was condemned. For the fall crippled him, but did not kill him outright. Who can say how many hours he lingered there on those lonely wind-swept rocks? At first, stunned by the fall, weakened by loss of blood, the time went by unconsciously; then he would collect his thoughts, remember how you thrust him down over the precipice in a moment of passion, and he would feel sure of your repentance and assistance. Did you hear no voice calling up to you?"

"The wind drowned every cry," said the sick man; and drops of sweat stood upon his forehead, and trickled down his face.

"But cannot you imagine how he kept expecting you, — expecting that you would seek help, let down ropes, come down yourself to save the friend you had loved? Or that you would hasten into Hardsmouth, get a boat, come round by the coast?"

"It was a night of storm," said Scott; "no boat could have lived in such a sea."

"But Michael lived through the night. He must have crawled up to the spot where I found the corpse, otherwise he would have been washed away. Think of the lonely and awful day succeeding that night, as he lay there dying of exposure, of loss of blood, of want of aid. Picture the pain of that utter abandonment. Too weak to call for help, too weak at last to move, and the crows gathering round him to stare into his glazing eyes. But he could think, and his thoughts could not have been such as to solace him. What had he to think of? The treachery of a friend, — a friend who, having murdered him, was not likely to stick at blasting his good name. He must have foreseen the specious tale you would get carried to the girl he loved; foreseen that she would believe he had deserted her, and so give her hand to his murderer. Perhaps he foresaw you in just such a life as you have led, honored and happy, while he, cut off in the heyday of youth, went down to an unknown grave. If he cursed God then, in the agonies of his abandonment, who can blame him? Yet, according to you and people of your creed, he thereby lost his soul, and so will suffer eternally, while you, in spite of your crime, because you have had time and opportunity to repent and obtain forgiveness, will die and go straight to life eternal. You may please yourself by calling this an expiation. I can only see in it an aggravation of the unfairness of your lot and his."

O'Brien watched the anguish in his victim's face with a keen pleasure at his heart; but down deeper still was an even keener pain, for he had come to love David Scott as much as one man can love another; and nevertheless felt bound to conceal his love and show hatred, because of the oath he had sworn. Bitter words were all that remained to him now he had abandoned bitter vengeance; yet he despised himself for bending to handle such woman's weapons.

Scott leaned his head upon his hand.

"To die alone . . . yes, it must be hard," he murmured; "human sympathy in that last hour is what the whole soul longs for. And Michael had none. No, I have not expiated."

An idea struck him. His mind was so unhinged, he believed it came from God. But to carry it out he must be alone.

"Will you leave me a while?" he asked; the pain here " — he pressed his side — " is so terrible . . . there is a remedy I must try. Perhaps in the garden you may find Catherine; you will wish to bid her good-by . . . but then return to me here . . . by yourself."

In moody silence O'Brien opened the French window and stepped out. Then Scott, unlocking a drawer in the table beside him, produced a small pistol, and laid it on the desk.

VIII.

At the same moment a gentle knock came to the door, and Scott knew it was Catherine's touch. He drew a newspaper over the pistol, leaned back again among the pillows, and, making a strenuous effort to compose his voice, called her in.

Never had she looked so sweet and winning; but Scott knew these loveliest blushes were not for him.

"Mr. O'Brien, father, is walking in the garden," she began. "I saw him from my window. Ought I not — Shall I go out to him?"

"Yes, go out to him, for he has come to take leave of us, Catherine. He is going away."

"Away!" repeated Catherine, amazed. "Where? Why?"

"He is returning to America."

"But only for a visit? He will come back?" she insisted, with varying color.

"No, dear one, I think — I fear he is going away for good."

Catherine looked at her father with those speaking eyes, which had long ago told him the secret she had thought so well concealed. But now it trembled on her tongue also. She opened her lips, hesitated, but could not frame the words.

O'Brien came in sight of the window, crossing the end of the lawn. He was deep in thought, but evidently Catherine had no share in it. He gave no glance towards the house, nor round about him, as he must have done had he been hoping to see her. One hand was carried behind his back, now loosely closed, now vehemently clenched; the other held his stick, which he prodded viciously into the ground as he walked.

Scott's eyes followed Catherine's, fell upon this figure; and despair seized the father, a forlorn hope awoke in the girl.

"Father, I love him," she said, looking up bravely.

"I have known it long, dearest."

"Did he say nothing?" — this very wistfully.

"Nothing you would care to hear He spoke of his journey — and of other things. He is a man whom grief and injury have rendered hard; he has no thought for softer feelings."

"Yet, if he had cared," said Catherine, "it would have pleased you too? For you like him, father?"

Scott gave no reply; yet he loved O'Brien and Catherine to that degree, he had come to the determination then and there to put an end to his life, that thus, by avenging Michael, he might remove the impediment between them.

Catherine pursued her train of thought.

"Do you remember what you said to me one night in the spring, as we drove home from town? It was a few days before I first met him."

That was the epoch-making day of her life, and every event was dated before and after.

"What did I say, Catherine?"

"You said that a woman should not be afraid to show her affection; that sometimes she might miss happiness by hiding it too well; that sometimes — you know — a man might be in love with a girl — and be too proud to show it — unless she — Father," said Catherine, lifting a pale and piteous face, "I love him so passionately that it is painful, there is a pain always here," — she pressed her hands upon her heart, — "I shall find no ease till he knows it. Day and night I am urged by a feeling I cannot explain, to tell him, although I hope for nothing, I ask for nothing in return. But unless I may speak I shall die! May I, father?"

Scott saw, in this unrequited passion of his Catherine's, the expiation demanded for her mother's levity, the last drop in his own cup of grief. But perhaps, too, he thought her innocent confession would touch O'Brien's heart, and when he should find also that Scott had made the final reparation, he would relent and be good to her.

"Go," said he, "if you must, and obtain, if you can, my pardon likewise. Good-by, my little daughter, God be with you."

Catherine went out into the garden and left her father alone.

IX.

SHE had heard his words of farewell, yet had attached no significance to them. Preoccupied with her own thoughts, she felt she had come to the supreme moment of her life, and the sudden meeting with Death himself could not have held more terror for her or more strange sweetness than this thing she was about to do. And as, too, at the hour of death, all false shame and all conventionalities drop away, and the soul at last comes near to other souls, as it never could do in life; so all the rules and teachings, all the arbitrary laws of society, slipped from her, and she listened to the voice of her heart instead.

O'Brien, turning at the end of the grass, saw her as she advanced towards him. He steeled himself to coldness.

Catherine gave him, for one instant, a chill and fluttering hand.

"You are going to leave us?" she said.

"Yes; my passage is booked for next week."

"But why do you go?"

"Why should I stay?" he replied roughly. "My business is finished; I have no other ties here."

"We had hoped, my father and I," said Catherine, "you would have found England so pleasant, you would not have wished to leave."

"Ah, of course!" he retorted bitterly. "Because you find life pleasant yourself, you imagine every one else should do so. It is a common mistake. You have a home, friends, many who love you, and so you are happy; but I have none of these things."

"Yet you might have them," said Catherine gently, "if you wished."

"That is a pretty speech. I suppose I ought to thank you? But I have lived a rude, uncivilized life too long ever to acquire the knack of giving and taking the pretty nothings of society."

The savage way in which he said this, the apparent anger that blazed from his eyes, did not daunt Catherine. On the contrary, it gave her courage.

"Mine was no pretty speech, and you know it," she answered. "If you go it is to please yourself, not because there are none here to regret you."

"If I thought you would regret me?" said he, tentatively; "but, no, I should be a fool so to deceive myself. You will forget me in a week. There is no one who cares for me."

His speech was framed with the cruelly deliberate purpose of learning more. He watched her closely to note its effect, and he saw how it awakened some strong emotion in the depths of her pensive eyes, how it changed the expression of her sweet and tremulous mouth, how it brought the vivid color rushing to her cheek.

But to herself she seemed to be lifted above time and space, to be standing with O'Brien in spirit only. She felt herself brave, and free to speak her inmost thoughts as only a spirit may.

"Do not say that no one cares for you," she began; "for there is a girl who loves you, and has loved you all along. Why should I be ashamed to own it? Does it do you any harm, or me any dishonor? I think it does me honor. I am better, prouder, and more glad since I have known you, than I ever was in my life before. And I ask nothing from you in return; only I could not let you go away without telling you. I said to myself, we are allowed to show our feelings of kindness, friendship, or admiration. Why then must love, which is best of all, be hidden forever in our hearts, as if it were something criminal? Let me tell you everything. At first you were always good to me. I thought that you liked me, and I tried to please you. Then you grew cold, and I was tormented, always wondering what was the reason. Sometimes I fancied if I had not been rich, you would have come nearer to me; and yet my heart told me that a man who loved a woman at all, would hold her far beyond and above her wealth. But then, when I heard just now you were going away forever, I felt I could not let you go in ignorance, for even where one cannot return the same affection, it is surely good to know oneself beloved. And I like to imagine that, in the days to come, when you yourself will love some good and beautiful woman, what I have told you will return to your memory and give you confidence. And do not think I shall be unhappy now when you have left me. I shall be happier all my life for having known you, and for having once, if once only, spoken the whole truth. And in proof of how much I trust you, I shall never, never regret what I have told you to-day."

O'Brien was looking at her with ardor. He had somehow got both her cold little hands in his. He pressed them passionately; and the girl, in spite of her last brave asseveration, was seized with fear. Her body trembled like a leaf, her face was suffused with blushes, she could not lift her eyes from the ground. At that moment she would have given the world to be away, anywhere out of his sight, out of the sound of his voice. She would have arrested perversely, had she been able, the words she so longed to hear.

"Catherine, my darling, my own darling, you have more than atoned," he said, in a voice strangely altered, for the man had grown young again; he had thrown away the burden of twenty years' hatred, and the vow that had bound his heart broke from it like a gossamer thread. "I have not deserved your love, but come, I too have much to tell you." And they wandered away, out of sight, amidst the trees.

X.

DAVID SCOTT knelt down by his desk with the pistol lying before him. In the strong sunlight which filled the room he looked what he was, — a dying man. All round him were evidences of his material success. Fine pictures hung upon the walls, handsomely-bound books filled the dwarf cases, richly-colored oriental carpets were spread over the floor. Through the window his eyes fell upon his own freehold acres, — upon the lawns and shrubberies which were his; upon the million-fanned chestnuts, the feathery acacias, the ever-rustling elms, which, planted so many generations ago by dead hands, had grown straight and strong to shadow the gardens for his use. He saw his daughter, conspicuous in her white dress, talking with O'Brien. The conversation between them seemed suddenly to grow intense. Catherine gesticulated unconsciously with her hands. He could guess from their motion, as well as from O'Brien's rigid figure and sunken head, how fruitless was her task.

Scott groaned. The physical pain he was suffering at that moment from the rapid development of his disease was nothing to his agony of mind. In the midst of luxury and every apparent condition for happiness, David Scott was as miserable in body and soul as any man that day in London. He clasped his

THE EXPIATION OF DAVID SCOTT.

hands, and the tears forced themselves down his sunken cheeks.

"O God and Father," he prayed aloud, "if I do this thing Thou knowest the purity of my motives. Not in despair, nor in contempt of Thy holy laws, do I take the life Thou hast given me, but to expiate the crime by which I took Michael's life from him, and left him to die alone without one friendly hand to moisten his lips with water, or wipe the death-dews from his brow. If in those last dreadful moments he doubted of Thy goodness, the fault was mine. If he came into Thy presence uncalled and unprepared, it is right that I too should in the same way seek Thy awful judgment seat, for hast not Thou said, 'An eye for an eye, a tooth for a tooth'? But towards my little girl, my Catherine — " The anguish of this thought was too much for the man; he laid his head on the table before him, and his prayer lost all coherency and purpose. For some moments his soul was in confusion. Then his hand touched the cold steel of the pistol, and it recalled to him his intention. He grew calm, rose from his knees, carefully looked to the loading of the pistol, and, holding it in his right hand, pressed the nozzle against his waistcoat, moving it a little this way or that as he felt for the heart below.

A shadow fell upon the window. Catherine stood without, and O'Brien looked over her shoulder. The girl pushed open the glass and came in. Her face was exquisite in its shy happiness. Scott had just time to put the pistol down unobserved on the table behind him, before Catherine reached her arms up round his neck, and laid her head upon his breast.

"Dearest," she murmured, "we are going to be so happy." Scott looked over the pretty, fair head to O'Brien. There was something in the man's appearance totally different to his ordinary self, and yet strangely familiar too.

"David," he said, coming nearer, and Scott's thoughts travelled mysteriously back to the days of Michael's lifetime, — "David, will you forgive me — for Catherine's sake — as I have forgiven you?"

A giddiness rushed over Scott. He had but time to put Catherine from his arms before the room turned round with him, wavered into blackness, and for an instant everything was blank. Then he stepped out of the darkness on to a sunlit cliff, where he and Michael were walking side by side; every step they took was on scented thyme and tiny golden colts-foot, two blue butterflies fluttered in arabesques over the ground, above was a blue and ardent heaven, below a blue and glittering sea. He tasted the saltness upon his lips, and the slumberous far-away sea-song hummed in his ears. Michael spoke to him, and he answered. At first it was solid, vivid reality. Then he came to know it was only his spirit there on the cliffs, that his body was lying back in his easy-chair in his own library, where busy hands were endeavoring to keep him captive, to cheat him of the vision. He resisted; his soul escaped once more; but the sunshine on the cliff was already paler, the flowers were drooping, the butterflies were gone. Michael's face looked strange and indistinct, yet his voice now sounded close at hand, in his ear.

"Davy, Davy!"

What did it mean? For surely he was again in his own library, struggling painfully back to consciousness.

Yes, it was the voice of the dead Michael; but it was James O'Brien who spoke, kneeling beside Scott's chair.

"Forgive me, Davy, dear old friend, forgive me; my sin has been greater than yours!"

From O'Brien's face the dark and sinister look was gone; his eyes had lost their coldness; emotion gave him back a reflection of his beautiful youth.

Over the dying man old memories crowded. Now, as he listened to him, he understood why from the very first this stranger had held such fascination for him.

"There never was a James O'Brien," said the speaker; "he was a figment of my brain, an instrument of my vengeance. For it was I who, lying crippled at the cliff's foot, was picked up by the crimps and shipped while still unconscious. During twenty years of exile I brooded revenge. I thought on our broken friendship, my lost Catherine, my ruined life, and my heart became a hell of evil thoughts. I sought you out with the determination of making you pay for every pang that I had suffered; and when I found you happy in your daughter, I conceived the plan of playing with her heart as the mother had played with mine. But from the first moment I saw Catherine, something more than the old love revived. I felt I could do her no wrong, so I made up my mind to leave. I meant to forego everything once more, — friendship, love, happiness, and my revenge as well. But Catherine has given me back all you once took from me, a hundredfold. Let her earn me, David, your pardon too."

Twilight fell upon the room for David Scott. Only dimly could he see the faces of the man and woman he loved; but holding a hand of each, in each of his, his feeble grasp tightened a little over them as he spoke.

"God has been very merciful to me," he said; "be good and happy, Catherine. Then he withdrew his hand from hers to lean over more completely towards O'Brien.

"Kiss me, Michael," he asked him; but almost before the kiss could be given and received, he had passed away without a sigh.

THE END.

THE KEYNOTES SERIES.

16mo, cloth. Each volume with a Title-page and Cover Design

By AUBREY BEARDSLEY.

Price, $1.00.

  I. **KEYNOTES.** By GEORGE EGERTON.
  II. **THE DANCING FAUN.** By FLORENCE FARR.
  III. **POOR FOLK.** By FEDOR DOSTOIEVSKY. Translated from the Russian by LENA MILMAN. With an Introduction by GEORGE MOORE.
  IV. **A CHILD OF THE AGE.** By FRANCIS ADAMS.
  V. **THE GREAT GOD PAN AND THE INMOST LIGHT.** By ARTHUR MACHEN.
  VI. **DISCORDS.** By GEORGE EGERTON.
  VII. **PRINCE ZALESKI.** By M. P. SHIEL.
  VIII. **THE WOMAN WHO DID.** By GRANT ALLEN.
  IX. **WOMEN'S TRAGEDIES.** By H. D. LOWRY.
  X. **GREY ROSES AND OTHER STORIES.** By HENRY HARLAND. [*In preparation.*
  XI. **AT THE FIRST CORNER AND OTHER STORIES.** By H. B. MARRIOTT WATSON.
  XII. **MONOCHROMES.** By ELLA D'ARCY. [*In preparation.*
  XIII. **AT THE RELTON ARMS.** By EVELYN SHARP. [*In preparation.*
  XIV. **THE GIRL FROM THE FARM.** By GERTRUDE DIX. [*In preparation.*
  XV. **THE MIRROR OF MUSIC.** By STANLEY V. MAKOWER. [*In preparation.*

Sold by all Booksellers. Mailed, postpaid, on receipt of price, by the Publishers,

ROBERTS BROTHERS, BOSTON, MASS.

John Lane, The Bodley Head, Vigo Street, London, W.

Messrs. Roberts Brothers' Publications.

THE GREAT GOD PAN AND THE INMOST LIGHT.

BY ARTHUR MACHEN.

KEYNOTES SERIES.

16mo.   Cloth.   Price, $1.00.

A couple of tales by Arthur Machen, presumably an Englishman, published æsthetically in this country by Roberts Brothers. They are horror stories, the horror being of the vague psychologic kind and dependent, in each case, upon a man of science who tries to effect a change in individual personality by an operation upon the brain cells. The implied lesson is that it is dangerous and unwise to seek to probe the mystery separating mind and matter. These sketches are extremely strong and we guarantee the "shivers" to anyone who reads them. — *Hartford Courant.*

For two stories of the most marvelous and improbable character, yet told with wonderful realism and naturalness, the palm for this time will have to be awarded to Arthur Machen, for "The Great God Pan and the Inmost Light," two stories just published in one book. They are fitting companions to the famous stories by Edgar Allan Poe both in matter and style. "The Great God Pan" is founded upon an experiment made upon a girl by which she was enabled for a moment to see the god Pan, but with most disastrous results, the most wonderful of which is revealed at the end of the story, and which solution the reader will eagerly seek to reach. From the first mystery or tragedy follow in rapid succession. "The Inmost Light" is equally as remarkable for its imaginative power and perfect air of probability. Anything in the legitimate line of psychology utterly pales before these stories of such plausibility. *Boston Home Journal.*

Precisely who the great god Pan of Mr. Machen's first tale is, we did not quite discover when we read it, or, discovering, we have forgotten ; but our impression is that under the idea of that primitive great deity he impersonated, or meant to impersonate, the evil influences that attach to woman, the fatality of feminine beauty, which, like the countenance of the great god Pan, is deadly to all who behold it. His heroine is a beautiful woman, who ruins the souls and bodies of those over whom she casts her spells, being as good as a Suicide Club, if we may say so, to those who love her ; and to whom she is Death. Something like this, if not this exactly, is, we take it, the interpretation of Mr. Machen's uncanny parable, which is too obscure to justify itself as an imaginative creation and too morbid to be the production of a healthy mind. The kind of writing which it illustrates is a bad one, and this is one of the worst of the kind. It is not terrible, but horrible. — *R. H. S. in Mail and Express.*

Sold by all Booksellers.   Mailed by Publishers,

ROBERTS BROTHERS, BOSTON, MASS.

Messrs. Roberts Brothers' Publications.

DISCORDS.

A Volume of Stories.

By GEORGE EGERTON, author of "Keynotes."

AMERICAN COPYRIGHT EDITION.

16mo.   Cloth.   Price, $1.00.

George Egerton's new volume entitled "Discords," a collection of short stories, is more talked about, just now, than any other fiction of the day. The collection is really stories for story-writers. They are precisely the quality which literary folk will wrangle over. Harold Frederic cables from London to the "New York Times" that the book is making a profound impression there. It is published on both sides, the Roberts House bringing it out in Boston. George Egerton, like George Eliot and George Sand, is a woman's *nom de plume*. The extraordinary frankness with which life in general is discussed in these stories not unnaturally arrests attention. — *Lilian Whiting*.

The English woman, known as yet only by the name of George Egerton, who made something of a stir in the world by a volume of strong stories called "Keynotes," has brought out a new book under the rather uncomfortable title of "Discords." These stories show us pessimism run wild; the gloomy things that can happen to a human being are so dwelt upon as to leave the impression that in the author's own world there is no light. The relations of the sexes are treated of in bitter irony, which develops into actual horror as the pages pass. But in all this there is a rugged grandeur of style, a keen analysis of motive, and a deepness of pathos that stamp George Egerton as one of the greatest women writers of the day. "Discords" has been called a volume of stories; it is a misnomer, for the book contains merely varying episodes in lives of men and women, with no plot, no beginning nor ending. — *Boston Traveller*.

This is a new volume of psychological stories from the pen and brains of George Egerton, the author of "Keynotes." Evidently the titles of the author's books are selected according to musical principles. The first story in the book is "A Psychological Moment at Three Periods." It is all strength rather than sentiment. The story of the child, of the girl, and of the woman is told, and told by one to whom the mysteries of the life of each are familiarly known. In their very truth, as the writer has so subtly analyzed her triple characters, they sadden one to think that such things must be; yet as they are real, they are bound to be disclosed by somebody and in due time. The author betrays remarkable penetrative skill and perception, and dissects the human heart with a power from whose demonstration the sensitive nature may instinctively shrink even while fascinated with the narration and hypnotized by the treatment exhibited. — *Courier*.

Sold by all Booksellers.   Mailed by Publishers,

ROBERTS BROTHERS, BOSTON, MASS.

KEYNOTES.

A Volume of Stories.

By GEORGE EGERTON. With titlepage by AUBREY BEARDSLEY. 16mo. Cloth. Price, $1.00.

Not since "The Story of an African Farm" was written has any woman delivered herself of so strong, so forcible a book. — *Queen.*

Knotty questions in sex problems are dealt with in these brief sketches. They are treated boldly, fearlessly, perhaps we may say forcefully, with a deep plunge into the realities of life. The colors are laid in masses on the canvas, while passions, temperaments, and sudden, subtle analyses take form under the quick, sharp stroke. Though they contain a vein of coarseness and touch slightly upon tabooed subjects, they evidence power and thought. — *Public Opinion.*

Indeed, we do not hesitate to say that "Keynotes" is the strongest volume of short stories that the year has produced. Further, we would wager a good deal, were it necessary, that George Egerton is a nom-de-plume, and of a woman, too. Why is it that so many women hide beneath a man's name when they enter the field of authorship? And in this case it seems doubly foolish, the work is so intensely strong. . . .

The chief characters of these stories are women, and women drawn as only a woman can draw word-pictures of her own sex. The subtlety of analysis is wonderful, direct in its effectiveness, unerring in its truth, and stirring in its revealing power. Truly, no one but a woman could thus throw the light of revelation upon her own sex. Man does not understand woman as does the author of "Keynotes."

The vitality of the stories, too, is remarkable. Life, very real life, is pictured; life full of joys and sorrows, happinesses and heartbreaks, courage and self-sacrifice; of self-abnegation, of struggle, of victory. The characters are intense, yet not overdrawn; the experiences are dramatic, in one sense or another, and yet are never hyper-emotional. And all is told with a power of concentration that is simply astonishing. A sentence does duty for a chapter, a paragraph for a picture of years of experience.

Indeed, for vigor, originality, forcefulness of expression, and completeness of character presentation, "Keynotes" surpasses any recent volume of short fiction that we can recall. — *Times,* Boston.

It brings a new quality and a striking new force into the literature of the hour. — *The Speaker.*

The mind that conceived "Keynotes" is so strong and original that one will look with deep interest for the successors of this first book, at once powerful and appealingly feminine. — *Irish Independent.*

Sold by all booksellers. Mailed, post-paid, on receipt of price by the Publishers,

ROBERTS BROTHERS, BOSTON, MASS.

LIBRARY OF DAVIDSON COLLEGE

Books on regular loan may be checked out for **two weeks**. Books must be presented at the Circulation Desk in order to be renewed.

A fine is charged after date due.

Special books are subject to special regulations at the discretion of the library staff.